JASPER'S BEGINNING

THE ATHERIAL ALLEGIANCE
BOOK 1
JASPER'S BEGINNING

DALTON R. BROWN

Dalton R. Brown
Missouri, USA

ISBN 978-1-7348215-0-5 (*paperback*)
ISBN 978-1-7348215-1-2 (*ebook*)

Cover design by: rose_miller
Printed in the United States of America

◇◇

*This book is dedicated to that little boy in elementary
school who, when he wrote his first story, knew he wanted
to be a author when he grew up. This book is for you.
You did it!*

◇◇

CHAPTER ONE

The night was cold, and the air was crisp, as it usually was this time of year. While others may not enjoy this type of weather, it didn't bother Jasper. If he was being honest, he quite enjoyed it. Jasper wasn't out tonight for leisure though. No, he was out for something more important. He was out to perform The Ritual of Protection. As it was so eloquently named, The Ritual of Protection was an annual event. This meant that every year, and it had to be exact, the wards had to be recast for the safety of the clan and its people.

This was Jasper's eighteenth year of life and his third year of being charged with the responsibility of performing it. He had been doing so since shortly after being given full control of his basic powers, at sixteen. Children came into their powers around the age of puberty, but it was a traditional rule that they were not given full control until they turned sixteen. Even then, they still had a lot of training to do before they were able to realize their full potential.

Jasper had been the youngest clan's mate to be chosen to perform The Ritual of Protection. It came as a surprise to many that he was selected to do it. Usually, it was one of the Elders that performed the ritual. Being as they were some of the strongest and wisest of the clan. Needless to say, it had caused quite the stirrings in the community. After the success of his first year, though, those stirrings quickly died out. For everything its reason, or at least that is what his dad would say.

Jasper had been selected for the role he was in because his basic powers were stronger than those of the other members his age, and even a good portion of those older than him. As for his full potential, that still remained a mystery to him. Jasper attributed this strength to his father continually working with him and allowing him to study spells above his age level.

Jasper stood in the field and closed his eyes. He felt the wind breeze past his face and blow his cloak around behind him. He was grounding himself, connecting with the earth and the energies that surrounded him. To be able to do this ritual, Jasper had to be sure to also cleanse any negativity that may be attached to him. This included the negative thoughts that he sometimes had about himself. While Jasper was thought of highly within his community, he didn't think he had done much to deserve such high praise and was continually finding faults within himself. This was always a good time for him to acknowledge those thoughts and accept his flaws for what they were.

He waved his hands above the moss-covered tree stump standing in front of him. The stump began to grow, twist, and shape itself into a beautiful tree-shaped altar. Jasper slowly glided his hand above the altar, right to left. As he did this, all of his materials and his book appeared. He started going through his things to gather what he would need for the ritual. The items called for were birch, vervain, heliotrope, sandalwood, and fluorite. After collecting the necessary items, and setting them to the side, Jasper waved his hand back over the altar. Everything vanished like it was never there to begin with. The altar then began to shift and shape itself some more. The once flat surface was now forming a bowl shape in the center of it. Jasper snapped his fingers, and the bowl started to fill with water.

Jasper watched as it filled and stared into it, looking at his reflection. He had shaggy, wavy, light brown hair with hints of blonde hidden throughout. Most days Jasper tried to keep it styled, but sometimes it was just too much to work with. On those days, he would just go about his day with how he woke up. Today, due to its importance, he took the time to fight with it. His face was thoughtful yet sincere, soft yet angular. His eyes were hazel with little golden specs hidden in them. His body was toned, though he didn't show it much.

Jasper looked up to the clear night sky. The light from the full moon shined down back at him, highlighting the angles of his face and the golden drops in his eyes. The moon was rising in on its proper place. It was almost time to begin. Jasper double checked to make sure his ingredients were ready. He then cast a circle using the stones placed around him and the altar.

As the moon got closer into its correct position, things began to quiet down. Jasper always enjoyed this part. It was like during this moment, and this moment alone, it was just him and the universe. Everything else just seemed to blur into the background. Jasper took in a deep breath and started the incantation.

"Testis maiorum Zephyra. Da mihi potestatem. Ostende mihi viam. Custodire ab nocere. Malum non transiet. Benedicite tutela ritual." He chanted. Which roughly translates to, I call upon the ancestors of clan Zephyra. Give me the power. Show me the way. Protect us from harm. No evil shall pass. Bless this Ritual of Protection.

Jasper continued chanting the words over and over as he placed the ingredients in the water. He slid his fingers along the sandalwood. As his fingers reached the tip of the incense, it began to burn. Jasper set the lit sandalwood into the water. It started to glow. As his chanting continued, Jasper could feel power building inside of him. His body began to pulse. He could sense the clan's ancestors giving him their power.

Jasper began to let the energy inside of him flow out. It started at his palms and began wrapping around his hands until they were ablaze with glowing blue energy. His eyes changed to the same blue color. Whenever anyone began to use their energy, their eyes were the first thing to change.

He stood in the middle of the circle and held his arms out to his sides, parallel with the ground. As he spoke the incantation one last time, he brought his arms above his head with a forceful clap. The energy traveled down his arms to his chest. The pull of the moon accepting the energy was so strong that Jasper began to lift off the ground. His arms fell down as the energy escaped from his chest, which was now arched. It shot all the way up to the sky, striking the moon.

Jasper remained floating and out of breath as he looked up at the moon. He watched as it soaked up the energy he had sent. The moon began to grow brighter and brighter until it sent out a pulse from all around it. Then it shot back down a beam of pure white energy that dove straight into Jasper, where his energy had just left. Once it struck him, the force sent him back down to the ground. He landed on his back, feeling the energy enter his body. It traveled through him, exiting into the earth. Jasper was exhausted, this was always his least favorite part. The ritual was complete though, and his people were safe. His duty was fulfilled. Jasper laid there on his back and looked up at the night sky. He was still connected with the moon and the ancestors, but the link was fading.

As he continued to look up at the moon and stars, he could hear the whispers of the ancestors. It was the usual whispers of positivity and protection. He had never told anyone about this part of the ritual, this part was his and his alone. Jasper was filled with pride. He took some time to reflect on his earlier memories. One of his fondest was of his father teaching him the correct way to say Zephyra. Jasper had always said 'Zeph-ur-a,' it took him a while to be able to understand it was 'Zeph-ear-a.' As the voices quieted down, he thanked them all and closed his eyes to regain his strength for the walk home.

Jasper stretched and rolled over to pick himself up off the ground and shook out his cloak. He adored this cloak. It was given to him by his father when he graduated from school. It was a deep dark sapphire blue, lined with black on the edges which were separated from the blue by gold and silver threading. The inside of it had been enchanted so that it reflected the night sky and beyond. On cloudy nights, when the sky wasn't visible to the naked eye, Jasper would pull out his cloak and just get lost in thought staring at it and all the wonders it reflected back to him. There was just something about it that called to him.

Jasper slipped on his cloak and walked over to the altar, which was still full of water and the other items he had used. Jasper looked into the water and chuckled at his reflection. His once styled hair was now a mess from all the energy coming and going from him, plus the whole laying on the ground part didn't help matters much. He debated on fixing it, but decided he actually quite liked it. He watched as the blue energy faded from his eyes and they turned back to their normal state. It would be a bit before he could use any big magic, but it was always worth it to know that his clan was safe.

Jasper grabbed the stone from the water and stashed it into a bag. He placed the bag into one of his pockets. He then dug a hole in the loose soil around the altar and buried the supplies to give back to nature for helping him. He finished up by waving his hand over the altar and watched as it shifted back into the mossy tree stump it once was. Jasper turned around tired, but also proud, and started his walk home.

Everyone would be back there waiting for him to celebrate another year of a job well done. As he walked down the wooded path, he could catch glimpses of a bright light glowing in the distance accompanied by loud noises.

"They must have started the fire and celebration without me." He said to himself, wondering how long he had laid in the field listening to the ancestors speak to him.

As he got closer, a sense of panic started to rise inside of him. He began to walk a little faster. The cries he had assumed were cheers of joy and celebration turned to screams of panic and fear. Jasper took off running.

Jasper ran out from the woods to the main grounds, where he saw the clan hall was ablaze. The once beautiful castle was now burning and crumbling down to the ground. The panic inside him grew. Where was everyone? Where were the guards? That's when he noticed the piles of ashes lying all over the place. His heart dropped to his stomach. Was one of those piles his dad? Who was attacking them? They should all be safe. The ritual was complete. Why was this happening? Jasper's head was spinning with all types of thoughts and concerns. No, he couldn't think like that. He had to stay focused and positive. He could hear fighting in the distance. There was still hope. So he took off, hoping for the best but preparing for what he might see.

Jasper rounded the corner of the corridor and found Kato Alazon, the clan leader, throwing blasts of energy at an enemy. Jasper couldn't see who it was, they were hidden in a cloud of dense smoke. How was this possible? Kato, who was also his father, noticed Jasper's arrival.

"Jasper, run!" He shouted, throwing another energy blast.

The shrouded figure laughed as a burning ball of fire grew above them. They were saying something, but Jasper couldn't make it out. Then, before Jasper could even react, it came flying straight at him.

Jasper shot up from the ground, still sitting in the circle he had cast. The whispers of the ancestors were no more. There was only him and the sound of his racing heartbeat, or so he thought. In front of him stood a beautifully divine woman. She had a light tan on her skin. She was wearing a flowing white gown that blew in the wind, almost weight-lessly. Her deep black hair was long and wavy, and flowed down her back. As she walked closer, it seemed to carry a dark blue tint and had shiny specs hidden all through it. It too was blowing in the wind, covering parts of her face. Jasper could barely make out her eyes. They shimmered back at him, silver, highlighting the specs in her hair.

As she walked closer, he noticed there was, in fact, no wind blowing. She started to speak, her voice was calming but sounded hushed and echoed.

"You have seen what is to come. You must stop the imminent threat if you want to avoid this destruction." She reached out her arms to help up the overwhelmed Jasper off of the ground, "Now go. Hurry, and save them all."

Then just as quickly as she had appeared, she vanished from his sight. Jasper stood there, unable to process what had just happened. He didn't know what parts, if any, were even real. Jasper turned around to start heading back, filled with worry and dread. As he headed down the path, he saw bright lights in the distance and took off running.

CHAPTER TWO

Jasper continued running, not stopping until he reached the clan's walls. As he approached the open gates, he could smell something burning. He burst through the gates prepared for the worst, but there everyone was. They were singing and dancing and having a joyous time. No one even noticed the way he entered the grounds, well almost no one.

"What's with the face?" Kato asked as he approached Jasper, "You look like you've seen a ghost."

Kato chuckled as he took a sip from his gold-rimmed goblet. Kato was double Jasper's age, but he managed to maintain his youthful look. He had medium blonde hair, which he always wore back. His heavy robe was white, with jewels lined around the edge. His face was more angular than Jasper's, but his mannerisms were always kind. His eyes were light green with shades of a darker color spread all around. His body type was also more mature looking than Jasper's. Where Jasper was toned, Kato was muscular. Should anyone challenge him, they'd be in for a fight for sure.

"Oh, you know," Jasper caught his breath and fixed his posture to something more relaxed, "I didn't want to miss the festivities. After all, it's not every day we get to celebrate like this. The big mean clan leader tends to be a bit of a stickler." He replied with a chuckle of his own, as he nudged his arm playfully into his father.

"Thank you, Jasper." Kato gave him a hug. As he let go, he looked down and smiled at Jasper, "I don't know what Zephyra's future would be like if we didn't have you. You may not be of my blood, but don't ever think that means I think of you any differently. You are my son, and you make me a proud father."

Jasper hugged him back. He hadn't known much about his birth parents, only that they died in a battle between clans. Kato took him in as a baby. He was the only father that Jasper had ever known. There was no way Jasper was going to ruin this night with what he had seen. For all he knew, it could have just been a dream. It had to have been a dream, right?

The rest of the night was spent dancing, singing, and celebrating the peace that was to come for the clan. Jasper tried hard to empty his mind of what he had seen. While he was able to celebrate, he just couldn't shake the visions. He decided tomorrow he would have a sit down with his father and tell him about everything that had happened. If anything, just to have him say it was all nonsense. Jasper chose to leave the celebration early and headed home to go to bed.

Clan Zephyra got its name from the being who trained the original and founding members. Zephyra, as the mysterious woman was named, was in search of pure souls to help fight away what she only called the darkness. She helped them to harness and understand their inner power. Once they were trained, she created a hidden piece of land. No other mortal would be able to find it, only those chosen by the clan members would be allowed in. Then, just as quickly as she had entered their life, she left. Nothing is known about Zephyra's origin, or why she helped create the clan. All she ever said was that they were needed to fight the coming darkness, and to always take in those who seek shelter.

As time went on, and more people were brought in, the clan became its own community. They shut themselves off from the outside world and focused on harnessing their powers to fight for the light. They built a castle which acted as the clan hall. As space became sparse, they began building housing on the castle grounds. It was around that time, they decided to give their community a name. After much deliberation, they settled on that of Lyteshaed.

While some rules would change over time, they thought it best to keep some things the same. The clan leader became Chancellor of Lyteshaed, while the Elders remained their advisors. Slowly members began to integrate back into the outer world, but the leader and their family were to remain living on the lands. This was for both their protection, and the community's.

Kato came from the long bloodline of rulers of Lyte-Shaed. It was always the firstborn who carried on the duty of being the leader. The rest of the family would take on other roles, some would teach, some would fight, some would go on to become Elders. Kato had been the only child born from his parents. His mother passed down the role to him on his eighteenth birthday. Ever since then, he has been doing the best he can to continue to lead his people to victory against the dark forces that threaten this world.

Whenever the clan had a big gathering like this, some people would stay in the castle while others would remain on the grounds in guest housing. The effects of anything cast would go with you as long as you were there when rituals were performed, but it was always stronger in Lyteshaed. The castle was also open anytime you wanted to get away from the mundane world. Kato was big on trying to convince the clan to socialize and blend in. Even Jasper and Kato got out from time to time to explore the world. Ultimately, loyalties were tied to Zephyra, but Kato thought that having interests outside of the clan was healthy too. It would make them fight more for the light, and not let the darkness in.

As Jasper got close to the castle doors, he couldn't help but stop and stare at it. The images of it burning were still stuck in his mind. What was so strong that it could get through the protective shield of the ritual and burn the castle down? The Elders had cast wards on the castle, sacrificing some of their own life essences, to protect it from harm as the last result fail-safe. This castle had stood through many battles and wars. It's beauty still unmarked. Jasper loved the castle, it was his home. The thought of losing it was devastatingly heartbreaking. Even more so, was the thought of losing his friend.

The castle had a personality of its own. A spell gone awry had caused the castle to form its own life force. Even giving it the ability to corporealize a body of its very own, with a conscious and everything. Ever since then, the castle never looked the same again. Not only did it have its own consciousness, but its own powers too. Axton, as the castle's corporeal form preferred to be called, was always changing the outside and inside design and decor. Jasper had befriended Axton. A lot of hours alone, while his father was away, would do that. At this point, Axton was like family to Jasper. He couldn't imagine losing him.

"Hey Jasper, how'd it go?" Axton approached Jasper as he entered the castle.

Axton had created his body from that of those who he had seen enter his domain. He had a build similar to Kato's, but with an even more sophisticated look. His hair was black, with grey streaking on the sides. His eyes were a type of stone-grey color, his skin tone was much darker than Jasper's and Kato's. He wore a suit almost all the time.

Jasper had tried, many times, to get him to switch to a more relaxed outfit, but Axton does love his suits.

"You know, same as always. I'm just too drained to enjoy the celebration. Lots on my mind, I'd rather go to bed and forget it all." Jasper replied with a warm smile.

Axton nodded. He knew Jasper enough to know something was up but thought it best to let him speak up when he felt comfortable enough to.

"You're good." Axton smiled, "Go get some rest. See you tomorrow."

Jasper approached his room, wondering what it would look like. Axton only changed Jasper and Kato's rooms when they asked for it. Jasper had recently told him he was feeling a need for change. The inside of the castle had an exquisite look to it. There were many winding staircases, the walls were white with pictures of past clan members hanging, and the main floors were black tile. It was simple, yet classy. Would this be the style that carried over into Jasper's room? He opened the metal door and stepped into his room.

As he closed the door, he was amazed at what he saw. What was once metal, was now a dark brown solid oak. The wall in front of him was more window than it was wall, huge drapes hung in front of the windows. The wall to his right was a bookcase, top to bottom, with a large nook in the middle for tv and entertainment. On the left was a wall with his bed centered in the middle with a door on the far end. The doorway most likely led to his bathroom, he thought. His bed was huge, as it was custom made. It had pillars standing at each corner, holding a canopy of wrapped, see-through, colored cloth all around it. The ceiling was a huge glass dome with a view of the outside sky. Beside the door was a control panel, it controlled the drapes and also darkened the ceiling to keep the light out. Axton had done a fantastic job. Jasper would keep his room like this for a while. Later, he thought to himself, he would have to look for the secret room that was always hidden in a wing. Jasper loved secret rooms, and Axton did too. They tended to make a game out of it. In fact, Axton wouldn't change the castle design until Jasper found all the hidden rooms.

Jasper changed out of his clothes and got into bed. His bed was so comfortable. It wrapped around him like a welcoming hug, and felt like he was laying on clouds. Jasper laid on his back, staring through the cloth at the night sky. Now that he was alone, and away from everyone, he could take some time to think about everything. Who was that lady? Why would she have shown him something like that? Was any of it real? Could it be stopped? Jasper's head swarmed with so many questions, but his eyes were getting heavy. He reached over for the remote on his nightstand, which was a tree trunk with different little creatures and fae carved into and all around it. Axton really pays attention to details, he thought to himself with a grin as he clicked the remote to darken the ceiling and then fell into a deep uneasy sleep.

"Jasper, run!" Kato yelled as the fireball came hurtling

straight at him.

Jasper shot up in his bed, he was covered in sweat. He sat in bed, trembling and out of breath, trying to calm himself down. He was going to have to talk to his dad about this, and soon. Jasper had gone from telling himself it was just a bad dream, to wondering if he was honestly being shown visions of a very possible and real future. He couldn't let his people be attacked, he had to save them. But how?

Jasper got up and went to his bathroom to get ready. He hadn't checked it out last night because he was too stressed and tired. The bathroom itself was very large. There was a tub with jets and a walk-in shower. The shower was in a little area of its own, the walls and floor were black with glass doors leading into it. The tub was white and was built where you had to step up on a platform to get into it. The sink and mirror area were nice too. The whole wall was a big mirror, with a bar and two sinks evenly spaced on it. Jasper was, yet again, amazed by the work of Axton. He got undressed and got in the shower. The water running down his body felt good. It was like if he stayed in there long enough, maybe, it could wash his troubles and worries away too. Jasper knew that wasn't going to happen, though. So, after enjoying it for a bit longer, he finished up and got ready to go talk to his dad.

Kato was in his office, which is where he usually was. His office seemed to echo that of the rest of the castle. It was exquisite, full of old-world class and sophistication. There were tall windows on the back wall like Jasper's, but in a different style. Jasper's were window panes with minimal separation involved. The ones in here were the same size, but they had been divided into multiple small squares. There were sculptures and relics spread throughout the room. The walkway led straight to Kato's desk.

"Dad?" Jasper called out, looking around the room for his dad, "Where are you?" he could hear a rustling of papers and books in the distance, so he just followed the noise.

"Oh, Jasper." Kato jumped. He must have been buried in research, Jasper thought. "You startled me." He chuckled as he closed his books and motioned for Jasper to come and have a seat beside him. "What's on your mind, son?"

"Hey," Jasper walked over to his dad and sat down, "there's something I need to talk to you about. It's about last night."

"We all do crazy things in times of celebration." Kato chuckled and looked over at Jasper, "You know we're not a judging community. So, who was it? Who did you run off with?" He reached over and playfully slapped at Jasper's.

"No," Jasper chuckled, "it's not anything like that." Though, he thought to himself, it'd be easier if that had been the case. "Last night, after the ritual, something happened."

Kato's laughter quieted, and a grave atmosphere took over the room. He sat silently listening as Jasper told him everything about what had happened after the ritual. Well, almost everything. Jasper continued to keep the ancestor's whispers a secret. He couldn't see how it was tied into anything and didn't want to deal with the questions of why he had kept that fact hidden for so long.

Jasper sat there staring at Kato, prepared to be scolded for keeping this to himself. Instead, Kato chuckled.

"Oh, Jasper." He got up and walked over to kneel by his son, "You were really drained. You put a lot of energy into protecting Lyteshaed. It's only natural for you to be exhausted and slip into a dream state for a bit. But that is all it was, a dream. Your subconscious doubts came through and made you worry about the ritual. But we're all here and safe. Everything is fine" Kato got up, pulled his son up from his seat, and gave him a hug. "I hope this helped to ease your mind." He looked down at Jasper smiling.

"Thanks, dad." Jasper felt a wave of relief go over him, "I've just been so worried about this being a future event. I was worried I failed our people."

"Like I said, everything will be alright." Kato continued, "Why don't you go into town? Do a supply run and clear your mind. Maybe that'll help you." He hugged Jasper once more. Jasper nodded and left the office to get ready to head to town.

As Jasper walked out of the room, Axton walked in.

"Is everything okay?" Axton asked Kato.

"No." Kato sat down in his chair, his demeanor now changed, "No, Axton, everything is definitely not okay." Kato handed Axton an old worn journal, "He saw her last night." Kato paused, not wanting to acknowledge it, but knew he had to. "The Lady in White has contacted Jasper. It has begun."

CHAPTER THREE

Jasper assembled a list of items that he was running low on and got ready to go to town. Had Jasper been an average person, the trip to town would have taken him a while. Jasper wasn't an ordinary person, though, so his journey would be quick. It would be as quick as walking through a door, to be exact.

Kato set up a business in town to serve as a haven for clan members when they felt like they needed a place to go and get away. He named it Mystic Delight. It had another purpose as well. It served as a portal between town and Lyteshaed. It was a way to cut travel time out for everyone and made things easier. There was always a protector at the shop to ensure those who weren't allowed couldn't stumble into the portal by accident, or otherwise.

The only other way to fast travel to Lyteshaed was known exclusively to the Chancellor and the Elders. Jasper had overheard his father talking about it once, it's a sigil of some sort. It allows the caster to think of any destination, not just the castle or shop. Then all they have to do is walk through a doorway, and they'd be transported instantly. Jasper was always trying to snoop and figure out what the sigil was. He hadn't had any luck, as of yet.

With everything gathered, Jasper headed to the main hall. The portal was set up right beside the castle entry doors. Jasper opened the door and entered the portal. He was at the shop in an instant.

"Hey kid, how's it going? How's your dad?" Victor Colvin, the guard, greeted him.

Victor grew up with Kato and Jasper's parents. He had joined them in many battles and had the scars to prove it. Victor was one of the few people who chose to keep his battle wounds. There were creams and salves that could speed up the healing and take away scaring, but Victor felt he had earned his and wore them with pride. His hair had greyed and was shaved on the sides. There was a small scar that sliced diagonally down through the center of his chin. It was usually hidden by the scruff on his face, but one could occasionally catch a glimpse of it. Victor stood tall, and his shoulders were broad. He was quite menacing. His piercing, ice-blue eyes were always scanning the area. There was no way anyone was going to accidentally stumble through the portal on his watch.

"I'm good. Dad's fine too." Jasper closed the door behind him to seal the portal, "I just wanted to get out and clear my head." He smiled, "I'm also running low on supplies and need to restock."

"And when can I foresee your return?" Victor took his place back in front of the door.

"I'll probably be about an hour or so." Jasper mulled it over.

"Okay, sounds good. You know how to contact us if you need any assistance." Victor accepted Jasper's answer.

"Yes, Victor, but I'll be fine. Marcus will gather the supplies for me, and I am only going down the road." Jasper assured him and turned around, heading towards the front of the shop.

Marcus Hale, the shop's co-owner, was at the counter checking out a customer. To the townspeople, it was just a coffee shop and lounge area. To the clan members, it was a safety zone and supply shop.

"Hey," Jasper walked up to Marcus and smiled, "how's it going?" Jasper handed him the list, "I'm going out for a walk, so there's no rush."

Marcus was a couple years younger than Victor and was a few inches shorter too. Marcus carried himself in a charismatic way. His brown hair was full of loose curls. He almost always had a smile on his face, it was as if he was trying to combat Victor's constant scowl. Victor and Marcus lived together in Lyteshaed. It was only natural for Marcus to want to go with Victor when he got stationed at the portal entrance. In fact, it was Marcus who helped come up with the idea of a shop. Kato agreed to let Marcus go with Victor and had a living area built on top of the shop so they would feel more at home.

"Okay, sounds good." Marcus's light brown eyes scanned the list of items, "We should have everything you need. I'll have it in the back waiting for you when you return."

"Thanks, I'll see you guys later." Jasper nodded in appreciation and turned to walk out of the shop.

The town they were in was of a decent size. Jasper tended to stay away from the more populated areas, though, as it was all just too much for him at times. He was more interested in the ocean, which was just down the street from the shop. That was the reason Kato had picked the location. He knew how deep Jasper's love was for the ocean. It was his way of giving Jasper something to have when he was away on business.

Jasper walked down the street towards the beach. He loved to watch the people and how they interacted with one another. Every so often, he would pass a member of the clan. They would give each other a slight nod in passing, as recognition of one another. Jasper wasn't feeling the social scene at the moment, though, so he didn't stop to talk. He just wanted to relax and watch the waves for a bit.

Jasper was always excited to see the beach. As he got closer, though, he could see just how busy it was. The weather was beautiful, so it made sense that everyone would be out on a day like this. Jasper had a trick up his sleeve for times like this. He would be able to enjoy his time, but have the experience be quiet and relaxing.

Jasper headed towards the restroom area to change out of his street clothes. He quickly slipped in, making sure not to be seen. After he checked to make sure he was alone, he locked the door behind him. He then bent over, like one does when they are stretching, reaching for the ground. As he came back up, he slid his hands against his body. He went from wearing a t-shirt and pants to swim trunks, sandals, and a pair of shades to match. Jasper turned around and lifted up the sunglasses to check himself out in the mirror in front of him. He let out a smirk as approval of the outfit. He gave his left hand a little shake and conjured up a towel to sit on. Ready to enjoy his beach time, he unlocked the door and walked on out.

As he got to the bridge, which connected the sidewalk to the beach, he scanned the sandy area for a spot to sit and be at peace. When he found the perfect place, he made a straight line towards it. He was also being cautious, trying not to draw attention to himself. Sometimes Jasper would come to hang out and be social, or to feed his flirtatious side. Not today, though. Today was about him and clearing his head.

Jasper threw his towel out across the sand and sat down to get comfortable. Once he was situated, Jasper pulled a corner of the towel back and drew a sigil in the sand. He placed his hand over the sigil to let his energy charge it. Then he removed his hand, revealing the design he had just drawn. It was now filled with his blue energy. He pulled the corner back down to cover it up so no one could see it.

What he had done was mute all of the voices and

distractions around him. Jasper could no longer hear the shouting voices of people around him or the whistling of the lifeguards yelling at people who very clearly knew not to be in the area they were in. Now he would only hear the waves crashing against the sand, the birds flying above him, and the breeze blowing against him. Jasper took a deep breath, a weight lifting as he inhaled the fresh aroma of the saltwater. He sat there looking out into the water, watching everyone splash and play around. Jasper stretched and closed his eyes as he laid back on his towel. He laid there soaking up the warm rays, shooting down from the sun, and attempted to forget the images haunting his thoughts.

The experience of the ocean always had a calming effect on Jasper. It always seemed to help him empty his mind and just drift away. As he lay on his towel, he would occasionally glance and observe the other beachgoers. Jasper enjoyed watching the interactions of those around him. They, too, had their stresses and struggles. They were just like him. The only difference was that Jasper had access to powers that they did not. That wasn't even true either, though. Through teachings as a child, you were taught that everyone has power inside them and gifts of their own. The issue is that the outside world had bred and molded it out of society. Darkness had ruled at those times, and couldn't have everyone running around with the ability to challenge their orders.

For that reason, the clan had hidden away from the world and chose to work in secrecy. They remained in the shadows because now it would just cause hysteria to society. They vowed to stay unseen but to also protect those who cannot defend themselves from the darkness and its evil workings. Occasionally, a team would have to be sent out to save someone who managed to unlock and access their powers. They would bring them back to Lyteshaed to teach and recruit them to help work for the light. Some would be lost to the dark, but they never gave up the fight and search.

"You know," A female voice spoke to Jasper, "you could at least put in earbuds to make it look like your preoccupied."

Jasper didn't know where the voice was coming from. His sigil was supposed to block people out. Only those with power would be able to talk to him while it was in effect. Jasper sat up and looked around. He scanned the area, searching for a fellow member of his clan. He didn't recognize anyone in the immediate area, so he wondered who it could be.

Then, Jasper saw her. She was walking towards him with the biggest smile. She carried herself with a purpose. She was wearing a bikini with black palm trees on it, and the colors of the sunset splashed all throughout it. The curves of her body filled out the bikini. Her hair was long, full, and wavy. The color was brown with a touch of blonde and what, from a distance, looked like pink running through it. Her skin was flawless and had a perfect tan to it. As she got closer, Jasper noticed her deep blue eyes with shimmers of a lighter blue in them. They seemed cheerful. She wore a bracelet on her right hand that attached to a ring on one of her fingers and a gold necklace with a ring on it. Jasper sat there, stunned. Who was this girl, and why was she walking towards him? His pulse began to quicken. He had never seen her before, was she from another clan? To be able to spot his active sigil, she had to be.

"Uhm, hi?" Jasper said as he sat there, processing everything.

"Hey, how's it going? What's your name?" She said as she smiled, looking at Jasper.

"Jasper." He nodded, not knowing what else to say.

She stopped beside him, kneeled down, slid her hand across the sand, and conjured a towel of her own. Then she sat down beside him.

"So, what's with the privacy sigil? Isn't the point of being at the beach to interact with people?" She chuckled.

"I don't mean to be rude," Jasper, still off guard, replied, "but who are you?"

She looked at him and seemed puzzled for a moment, and then she started laughing.

"Oh, silly me. I should introduce myself. I'm Freya," She shifted her body to turn and face Jasper and held out her hand, "Freya Everly. I'm sorry to intrude, it's just been forever since I've met someone who is like me."

Jasper didn't understand, wasn't she part of a clan? To be able to spot him, she had to have had some training.

"Someone like you?" He asked, still not understanding what was going on, "Don't you have a clan?"

"Yeah, okay." She started laughing, "A clan." She jokingly mocked. Then her face changed to a more serious tone, "Wait. You're not joking, are you?"

Jasper shook his head back at her.

"You mean to tell me you really don't know?" She stared at him almost with a more concerned look.

"Know what?" Jasper asked. A sense of worry hit him. What was this girl talking about?

"You're -" She began to speak but then was cut off by a voice behind Jasper.

"Jasper, your dad has asked for you." A voice spoke behind him.

Jasper turned around to see who it was. It was Victor. He wasn't staring at Jasper, though. Instead, he was staring at the girl sitting beside him. The look on his face definitely was not friendly. If Jasper hadn't known any better, he would think Victor was about to attack her. Victor took his job as a protector very seriously and did not take kindly to newcomers.

"We should get you back to him." Victor insisted, never once taking his eyes off of the stranger.

Jasper looked over at the mystery girl.

"Oh, okay. Catch you later, Jasper." She was back to the bubbly, overexcited girl she was when she first came over.

"Okay, see you later. I guess." He said as he gathered his stuff and kicked sand over his sigil to deactivate it.

"Okay, kid," Victor held his arm out to let Jasper walk in front of him, "let's get you to your dad. You can come back and flirt another day." He teased, nudging Jasper as he walked by.

Jasper let out a fake laugh to not be rude, but couldn't help to wonder what was up with everyone. Why were they all acting so weird?

CHAPTER FOUR

"So, what does dad need?" Jasper asked Victor as they walked back to the shop. Victor didn't reply. Jasper looked over at him, he seemed to be lost in thought. "Uh, Vic? Earth to Victor." Jasper waved his hand in front of Victor's face.

"Oh, what was that? Sorry." Victor said, snapping out of whatever thought he had been lost in.

"Well, I had asked what dad wanted. But now, I'm wondering what had your attention that strongly." Jasper said, searching Victor's face for any answers.

"I was just lost in thought. Don't worry, it's nothing for you to concern yourself with." Victor replied, continuing to stare ahead, "Your dad didn't say what he wanted you for. He just told me to go get you and have you meet him."

Jasper nodded back. He wondered what was so important for his dad to call him back. After all, he was the one who sent him off to relax.

When they got back to the shop, Marcus was checking out a customer.

"Were you able to get everything I listed?" Jasper stopped at the counter and asked him.

"Yes, it's all bagged and in the back." Marcus pointed with his head as he finished checking out the customer he was with.

Jasper nodded and walked to the back of the store with Victor. Jasper grabbed his bags while Victor opened the door for him to walk through the portal.

"Thanks, Vic." Jasper forced a smile, "Catch you later."

Victor smiled at him, but Jasper saw a flicker of something in his eyes. He shrugged it off and continued through the door.

"How was the beach?" Axton greeted Jasper, taking the bags from him.

"Cut short." Jasper replied. "Do you know what dad needed for him to send Victor for me so quickly? Especially after him being the one to send me out for the day?"

"He didn't say." Axton said as he started walking off to put away everything Jasper had got while he was out.

Jasper just stood there, his stomach tied in knots. Axton was not a good liar, and Jasper could tell something was up.

"First, Victor, and now you?" Jasper said as he caught up with Axton.

"What do you mean?" Axton looked down to the ground.

"This, this right here." Jasper stated. "You can't even look at me. What's up with everyone?"

Axton turned to face Jasper. He looked remorseful as he stared at Jasper.

"It's not my place to say. Please respect that and know I care for you, but some rules I cannot break." He turned and started walking off again, leaving Jasper behind. "Your father is waiting for you in his study." Then he turned a corner and was gone.

Jasper was quickly getting agitated with all the secrecy that was going on. He went to his room to change out of his swim clothes and into something more comfortable. Jasper decided if everyone was going to be secretive with him and make him wait for an answer, then they could wait for him. He took a shower and took his time getting ready. After he was done, he grabbed his cloak and headed to his dad's study to find out just what was going on.

Jasper walked into the room, expecting to see an agitated Kato for being made to wait for a while. What he wasn't prepared for, was for some of the Elders to be waiting too.

"Well," Kato huffed, "thanks for finally joining us." He motioned for Jasper to come and stand by him.

"I apologize for running behind." Jasper composed himself as he walked past the Elders then turned and snarked at Kato, "I was just under the impression I was supposed to be away taking a break."

Kato shot him a glance, which told him now was not the time for acting out. Jasper took a breath and turned around to face the Elders with a smile.

"So good to see you all again. Forgive me for my asking, but what is the purpose of your visit so soon after leaving just the other day?"

"They are here because I called for them." Kato placed his hand on Jasper's shoulder.

"You called for them?" Jasper turned his head to look up at his dad. "Is everything okay?" Jasper knew his dad would not have called the Elders unless there was something that needed to be handled immediately.

"He has told us about what you have seen." One of the Elders stepped forth and removed their hood.

It was Zara Vardeau. She had been friends with Kato growing up, and was one of the youngest Elders. Her face was timeless and wise, her eyes a piercing blue. She had her black hair cut short in a pixie style. She wore a silver-leafed ear cuff on her left ear. Her frame was hidden in the cloak, but Jasper knew from past meetings that she was about his height with an athletic build. While the other Elders stuck with more traditional looks, she broke the mold and tried to stand out.

"After hearing your story," She approached Jasper, "he thought it best to contact us just in case it was a true premonition you were being shown."

"When I came to you, though, you said it was nothing to worry about." Jasper looked at Zara and then at Kato.

"I know, and I'm sorry about that. I thought it was best to try and protect you." Kato replied

"Protect me! Protect me from what?" Jasper questioned.

Kato looked down at the ground. He seemed hurt, upset even.

"From the truth." Zara stepped closer to Jasper. She walked over to Kato and placed her hand on his shoulder, "He needs to know. You've done a good job caring for him. But if he is to be prepared for what is ahead, then he needs to know. It's best if it comes from you."

"You're right." Kato sighed heavily.

Zara patted him on the shoulder, then slid her hand off of him. She turned and smiled, a sad smile at Jasper.

"We will leave you guys to talk." Zara said as she and the Elders walked out of the room.

"Dad?" Jasper said as he walked up to Kato, "What's going on?"

"Jasper." Kato turned around to face his son, "You are the most important thing to me. Everything I have done was in the interest of you. You were a gift I did not know I needed. You have blessed my life in so many magnificent ways. If I had to do it all over, I wouldn't change any of it." Kato's eyes began to water as he looked down at Jasper and touched his cheek.

"Dad, you're scaring me." Jasper stood nervously facing Kato.

Jasper and Kato were always open with one another. They hid nothing. There had been no secrets, emotions were never hidden. What could be so bad that had his dad looking like this? Jasper's stomach began to hurt as his worry set in. Seeing his dad fight back the tears in his eyes was causing him to begin to do the same.

"Whatever it is, I'm sure it's fine." Jasper went in to give his father a hug. Kato hugged him back tightly.

"What you have been told about your past is not entirely true." Kato said, releasing his hold on Jasper.

"Wha-" Jasper froze, "What do you mean?" Jasper backed away from Kato.

Kato had always been honest with him about not being his biological dad. That didn't change the fact that he was Jasper's dad, and Jasper was his son. When Jasper was younger and would ask about his parents, Kato would tell him the same story. His parents were close friends of Kato's. They had all gone through training and school together. When Kato took over as Chancellor, Jasper's parents became his trusted Left and Right Hands. When Jasper was born, it was only natural for Kato to be named as the chosen one to take Jasper should anything happen to them. Kato had accepted the task, with no question. Though he never thought he would have to fulfill that role. Then came the battle. They had gone through battles before and were always victorious. This battle, though, ended up being different.

During the battle, Kato was under heavy attack. Jasper's parents were trying to get him back to safety when the other side's leader rushed them. Before they could react, he had thrown a deadly energy blast. Jasper's dad jumped in front of it, shoving his mom out of the way. Jasper's mom screamed and sent out a wave of energy that slew the leader where he stood. His followers charged towards her to retaliate. Kato rushed to her side, she had used way too much energy in her attack. Kato quickly drew a sigil in the ground which threw up a shield around them, but knew it wouldn't last long. He tried to think of a plan, but Jasper's mom had already accepted her fate. She told him to take care of her baby, then touched his forehead teleporting him back to Lyteshaed. The rest of the clan's fighters defeated the dark clan. But Jasper's mom had used too much energy, and was not able to fight back anymore. She also was lost in the battle.

Jasper had always been proud of his parents. They fought to protect one another and, in the end, did what was best for the clan and the light. Their sacrifice saved Kato, which made them heroes in Jasper's eyes. That notion had helped him to grieve and move on in life. To be told he had been lied to, destroyed him. Kato took a step towards Jasper, he could see the hurt on Jasper's face.

"No!" Jasper stepped back, a tear ran down his face. "What do you mean not entirely true?"

"The story you were told when you were younger?" Kato began

"Just tell me." Jasper interrupted.

"Those events did happen." Kato continued.

Jasper looked at Kato, his anger declining and confusion setting in.

"I don't understand. Then what isn't true?" He asked.

"The people in the story," Kato walked closer to Jasper, who didn't back away this time, "they weren't your parents." Kato caught Jasper as he fell to the ground in disbelief.

"If they weren't my parents, then who are my parents?" Jasper asked, fighting to hold himself together.

"Some things," Kato helped Jasper stand again, "still remain a mystery to me." Kato motioned for Jasper to come and have a seat, "But what I do know, I will tell you."

Jasper felt betrayed, but he followed Kato and sat down. After all, this was Kato. He was the only father he had known. He had always taken care of, and defended, Jasper. There must be a reason why he kept a secret this important away from Jasper.

"Your parents came to Lyteshaed looking for protection." Kato explained.

"Protection? Protection from what?" Jasper asked.

"They had done something in secret that was not allowed, and they were being hunted for it." Kato cryptically answered.

"What did they do?" Jasper attempted to dig deeper.

"They got pregnant with you." Kato replied.

Jasper sat back in his chair. How could being pregnant with him be something that needed to be a secret? More so, why were his parents being hunted for it?

"So, who were they?" Jasper asked, trying to understand everything.

"Well," Kato sat back too, "That's where memories get

blurry."

"What do you mean?" Jasper leaned forward.

"The Elders allowed for them to have sanctuary within our castle. They stayed with us until your mom gave birth. After having you, they knew they needed to leave again. They also knew it was too dangerous to take you with them. That was when the plan was made. My Left and Right Hands, Clare and Stephen Loesett, would agree to take you in as their own. Your mother did something that changed the memories of everyone except them, myself, and the Elders. Everyone was to believe they were your true parents. What your parents also did to further protect you, wiped even our memories of who and what they were. They asked us to watch over and guide you. That we were not to tell you anything of your true birth until you reported being in contact with a lady in white."

"So, she was real?" Jasper's eyes widened.

"Yes." Kato nodded, "Sorry, I told you otherwise earlier. We had to prepare everything before we could tell you the truth."

Jasper had many questions, "So then why the false story? There were so many things you could have told me instead."

"Everything was going as planned." Kato smiled, "Clare and Stephen had taken to you instantly. They loved you so much." Kato's smile faded away and was replaced with a mournful stare, "Then we were attacked. Like I said, the battle really happened, and they were lost to it. It was easier for me to take you in and let that be the story you were told, than to risk anyone finding out the truth about you." Kato placed his hand on Jasper's.

"I understand why you did what you did, but it all still hurts." Jasper shifted away to let Kato's hand fall off him. "I just need time to work this all out."

"I understand." Kato dropped his head, then got up and walked to his desk, "I have something for you." He went through some drawers, then walked back over to Jasper. "They left this for you." He held out a wooden box with strange carvings all over it. "They said when we revealed everything to you, to give you this. That it would help you understand everything better. Don't worry, none of us have gone through it. They enchanted it, that way it would only open for you."

Jasper took the box from Kato. The carvings began to glow a deep blue, then the box clicked open. Inside was a leather-bound journal with a stone right in the center. Beside the journal was a cloth that had something wrapped inside of it.

"This is just all a lot right now." Jasper closed the box.

"I understand," Kato walked over and knelt down in front of Jasper, "but you've been preparing for this day for a long time now. You're ready, I know it."

"Dad," Jasper looked up at Kato, "I'm scared."

"I'm right here for you, like I always have been." Kato grabbed Jasper and gave him a hug, "That will never change." He stood up and brought Jasper up with him, "Take the box to your room. Take a moment for yourself. Then go through it. If you need to talk after, come and find me and I'll be ready to listen." Kato forced himself to change roles as Jasper turned to walk away, "Send everyone in, will you? I have much to discuss with them."

Jasper nodded and walked out of the room. Outside were Axton and the Elders, sitting and waiting.

"He's ready for you guys. If you'd excuse me." Jasper nodded and walked off.

They all knew he needed time to be alone, and knew they needed to talk with Kato. Once Jasper was fully filled in, things would be moving at a fast pace. Everyone needed to be prepared. Axton and the Elders nodded at one another, then walked into Kato's study to begin the discussion.

CHAPTER FIVE

Jasper closed his bedroom door and walked over to his bed with the box in hand. He sat down and placed it beside him. Everything Kato had just said still weighed on him pretty heavily. After believing in something for so long, was he really ready to know the truth? Jasper took a deep breath and opened the lid.

The journal had a clear stone on it. When he reached out to pick it up, it awakened and swirled with the same blue energy that the box had earlier. The journal clasp opened. Some sections were smudged from what Jasper assumed must have been teardrops. He began to read.

My dearest Jasper,

> *Where to begin? First, know that your father and I love you so very much. We are doing what we have to, to ensure your safety. We are not making this choice with a light heart.*

Jasper's tears hit the page. The love his parents felt for him was undeniable. To be able to put their wants aside and ensure his protection must have been hard for them to do. He understood why they did what they did. What he didn't understand is why they did it. He continued reading.

Jasper had taken in a lot of information. He wasn't from this world? What could that even mean? Where was he from? The even scarier question, what was he? It sounded like the lady he had seen before is referred to as The Lady in White. At least to those who do not know her true name. His parents said that he could trust her. Which was a relief because that meant he wasn't going crazy. It also meant the premonition could happen. He needed to tell his dad right away.

Jasper rushed to his father's study to tell him about what he read. When he entered, the Elders were still there talking to Kato. Once they noticed him, they quieted down and watched him walk up to Kato.

"Yes?" Kato asked.

"Dad," Jasper started, looking at Kato and then the Elders, "We really need to talk."

"I understand, I just need to fin-"

"Now!" Jasper cut him off.

The Elders began to murmur to one another.

"Jasper," Zara stepped forward, "we understand you are going through something right now. We are trying to be respectful of that, but there are still rules you should follow and respect."

"Respect?" Jasper snapped back before he even thought about it. "Lying, keeping secrets, falsifying stories, should I continue? How am I supposed to respect those who cannot admit where they have faulted?" Then he looked at Kato. "My dad is the only one to apologize for the actions he has made. I understand why everything happened like it did, but that does not gloss over the fact you all had parts to play in it too."

"Jasper!" Kato gasped.

"No, Kato," Zara stepped in, "he is right." She turned and faced the others. "He has done wonderful things for this clan. He has kept us protected, above many other things. He acknowledges and understands why we agreed to play our part, but he is right." The Elders nodded as Zara turned back to face Jasper. "We all here, and those of us who are not, offer our deepest apologies for keeping secrets from you. We ask for your forgiveness."

Jasper felt a relief go over him. It didn't change what had happened, and the hurt of everything was still lingering, but it was nice to know people felt sympathy for their actions. Sure, they did what they did to protect him, but it involved shady operations in the process. To hear them apologize helped. He nodded back to them.

"Now," Kato spoke up, Jasper turned to face him, "what was it you wanted to talk about. I think you have our attention." He joked to lighten the mood of the room.

Jasper explained what he had read to everyone. He kept some things to himself for the moment. He didn't tell them about the necklace, stone, or that the journal had more to it to be discovered. He also didn't mention the whole not from this world part, either.

"So, you see." He finished, "We need to figure out a plan for what to do to protect everyone."

"From what you have told us about your premonition," one of the other Elders stepped forward from the group, "it sounds like this hooded figure is targeting you specifically." It was Oscar Finley, "So, and it should go without saying," he gave the other Elders a knowing look, waiting for them to come to his same conclusion, "we should move you and not alert the clan. We would be risking a frenzy."

Oscar had always carried an aura of self-imposed superiority. He was one of the oldest Elders. He had lost his hair many years ago, and his face bore the signs of time creeping upon him. The way he looked at people was like he was, not so subtly, letting them know they were not worth his time. While Jasper respected Oscar, as he did the other Elders, he could not stand him one bit.

"But the vision happens here." Jasper tried to argue back.

"Yes, that is true. But that's because you would have never left the clan before this." Oscar looked at Jasper like he was a newborn baby, innocent and ignorant. "If this supposed attacker is truly targeting you, then they will strike where you are. If you're not here," he glanced around to everyone in the room once more, "then the clan should be safe." Oscar defended his previous statement.

"I don't know, I think Jasper has a point." Axton stepped forward to help Jasper. "His vision happened here, and the journal tells him to trust his vision from The Lady in White."

"Who asked the castle for its input." Oscar lashed back at Axton.

"Whoa, now hold on right there." Kato stepped forward.

"Kato, no." Zara stepped between an agitated Kato and a smirking Oscar. "I've got this." Zara knew if Kato lashed out at an Elder, there would be consequences, and there was no time for that. She turned and looked at Oscar, "You should be ashamed for that comment." She flashed a kind smile at Axton, "Axton has housed, and allowed us to have safety within these walls. He, not it, protects us. You should show him some respect."

Oscar began to open his mouth, but Zara turned to Jasper and began talking again before he got the chance to say anything in reply.

"Now Jasper, I have to say I do agree with Oscar on his thoughts. I know what you are saying, and I hear you, but we have to think for the clan too. If we told them everything, it would cause madness. Oscar was right about that much. We don't need to risk their safety. You should come to stay with Luca and me. It will allow us to plan and prepare. We will have the advantage of it being on our own terms, and it also gives our people a better chance at not being dragged into this." She turned and looked at Kato. "You know what I say is true."

"Jasper, I think she is right." Kato said.

"Dad?" Jasper turned and looked at Kato. "The vision, it happens here."

"Yes, but that could have been a subconscious detail that you added to the vision. It was easy for you to see the battle happening here because this is your safe place." Kato explained.

"I guess." Jasper sighed.

"Trust me. I don't want to send you away knowing what you have seen and that we have much to discuss. But it is also our duty that we must think about the protection of the clan. They are innocent in all of this and do not deserve the fate you have foreseen. If we have a chance to change it, even if it's just the location, then we have to try. This way, at least they will all be safe. We can figure out the rest as we go." Kato attempted to reassure Jasper.

"Yeah, but-" Jasper tried to argue back.

"Jasper," Axton interrupted, "Your dad and Zara may have a point. You need to do this to make sure we can protect as many people as we can."

Jasper stood there, not knowing which way to go. Everything was happening all at once. Yeah, he was upset with everyone, but that did not mean he wanted to leave them either. Maybe they had a point, though. If there was a chance to protect the clan from being attacked, then he owed it to them to be the one to leave and see that they stay safe.

"Okay, Zara, I'll go with you." Jasper gave in.

"Thank you, Jasper." Zara acknowledged the burden that had been placed upon Jasper, "We will leave and give you some time to say goodbye and get ready. I'll wait for you in the main hall." Then she and the other Elders walked out of the room.

"I'm proud of you." Kato said as Jasper turned to face him. "I know we have much to discuss, and we will. Once we have this taken care of, I promise, we will sit down and talk about everything." He grabbed Jasper and hugged him. "I love you."

"Come on, Jasper." Axton spoke up behind them, "Let's go to your room and get your stuff."

Axton walked Jasper to his room, both of them remained

silent. When they reached the room, Jasper spoke up.

"Most of this, I can just conjure if I need it." He said, "I'll take my cloak and this box for now, though."

"Actually," Axton turned to look out the windows in Jasper's room. "I have something for you too." He turned around with a brick in his hand. "I probably shouldn't do this." Axton waved his hand over the brick. It began to change and twist itself until there sat a silver bracelet in his hand, "Here you go." He handed the bracelet to Jasper.

"Thanks?" Jasper said, not sure what to think.

"Only a few people have been given a piece of me. If you ever need me, channel some energy into that bracelet and call for me." Axton instructed, "I will be able to come to you. I won't be able to stay too long at one time, but at least you'll have a part of home with you while you're gone."

"I don't know what to say." Jasper put the bracelet on and then hugged Axton. "Thank you, Axton. For everything you've done."

"Anytime." Axton gave him one last hug then let him go. "You should probably be on your way now. I'm sure Zara is waiting and ready to go."

Jasper nodded, too scared to stop and think about anything for fear he might change his mind. He grabbed his cloak and the box off his bed, and then took one last look at his room.

"Maybe when I come back, I can find the hidden room in here." He halfheartedly attempted to lighten the mood, then turned and walked out of his room.

"Ready?" Zara met Jasper, the other Elders had done left.

"Yeah, as ready as I'm going to be." Jasper took one last look at everything.

"You're doing the right thing, you know?" Zara sympathized.

"It doesn't make it any less hard." Jasper replied with a heavy heart.

Kato walked into the main hall, Jasper could see how much pain he was in. Jasper kept telling himself he was doing the right thing by leaving.

"Now or never." Jasper turned back to face Zara.

"Well, on the plus side, you're getting to see something only the Chancellor and the Elders know." Zara winked at him then began drawing the sigil on the door that would allow them to travel anywhere. It must have been approved for her to let him see, possibly as a gift from the Elders for everything he had been through. "Okay, finished. Let's go, see you on the other side." She opened the door and walked through.

Jasper turned back once more. Axton and Kato were standing beside one another watching him.

"Smile, guys. It won't be long, and I'll be back." They both smiled, he did the same. "Love you guys." Then he turned to face the portal.

This was it, things were changing so fast all around him. Was he ready for it? He took a breath and walked into the portal, the door closing behind him.

CHAPTER SIX

Jasper stepped out of the portal and into Zara's house. They were in her basement. It was unfinished with concrete walls. Jasper looked around. There were bookshelves everywhere, full of all types of books.

"You're more than welcome to go through them if you want." Zara said, getting Jasper's attention.

"Thanks." He replied, continuing to scan the rest of the room.

There were little antique wooden tables scattered throughout the room. They had books, different ingredients, parchment, crystals, all sorts of things sitting on them. The basement's aroma was a mixture of ancient texts, incense, and herbs.

"So, I take it you guys use the basement as your altar room?" Jasper chuckled, also kind of amazed at what a collection they had.

"Oh, this? This is nothing." Zara laughed, "Follow me." She said as she began walking upstairs.

Jasper followed behind her. It was odd, he thought to himself, he had seen Zara and Luca many times at Lyteshaed, but this was the first time he had been to their home. They came out into the kitchen, which had a modern theme mixed with a Victorian theme to it. There were silver appliances, wooden shelves hanging all around, and an island with pots and pans hanging above. At the other end of the room was a wooden kitchen table. It looked like it had some type of etchings in it, but Jasper couldn't make out what of. Jasper wanted to check it out more, but Zara continued walking. He figured he would have plenty of time to check it out later and continued following her.

From the kitchen, they went through a little walkway that connected them to the living room. The rest of the house continued the mixture of a Victorian and modern theme. There were lots of wooden pieces and accents, the stairs were wooden and wound up to the top floor. The house was also very earthy, there were plants and crystals everywhere.

"Your house is beautiful." Jasper said, still taking everything in.

"Thanks," Zara proudly smiled, "we try." She looked around, "Speaking of we, where has Luca gotten off too? Let me go look for him. Make yourself comfortable in the living room, if you'd like." Then she went upstairs to go search for Luca.

Jasper scoped everything out around him, it really was a pretty house. He went into the living room and took in his surroundings. There were more books, crystals, and other items throughout the room. Some of them looked like log-books of historical events, while others discussed theories, thoughts, philosophies, anatomy, gardening, astrology, and beliefs about what else is out there. There were some correspondence books, dictionaries, and other training books for different knowledge levels. They really did have quite the collection.

Jasper walked over to the couch and tried to get comfortable in his new environment. His head was spinning from everything that was falling apart all around him. Jasper sat the box from his mom on the coffee table in front of him. He opened the box and grabbed the cloth, which now he knew had a necklace wrapped inside of it. He unwrapped the necklace. It was gold, with jewels studded all around a hole in the center. It looked like it had ridges in it to hold something, but what. He looked down at the stone in the journal. Maybe they go together, he thought. He reached down to grab the stone.

"Well, I guess Luca is still out. He should be home shortly." Zara said as she walked down the stairs.

"Oh?" Jasper jumped, stuffing everything back in the box, "How has he been?" Jasper hadn't seen Luca in a while.

"He's been good." Zara replied, "How are you doing?" She came over and sat down by Jasper. "If you need to talk about anything, I'm right here."

"Thank you." Jasper sighed, "I appreciate the offer, but I think I just need time to myself. I need to let it all sink in and get adjusted."

"I understand." Zara placed her hand on Jasper's back, as to comfort him, "Just know the offer stands." She got up and grabbed her phone, "Let me go give Luca a call and see where he is at." Then she walked out of the room.

Jasper sat on the couch, letting everything run through his mind. There was a lot going on all at once. He had to find a way to channel through it all. Jasper laid his head back on the couch. As he was about to drift off, the front door opened and closed.

"Mom! I'm home!" A voice called out.

It was Luca. Jasper sat back up on the couch as Luca walked in.

"Hey." He said, waving his hand at Luca.

"Uh, hey?" Luca replied, "What are you doing here? Did I forget about some planned event or something?" he laughed to himself as he slid his hand through his wavy hair.

Luca was just a smidge shorter than Jasper. His hair was about the same length as Jasper's but dark brown, some might even argue more black than brown. His skin was olive, and his eyes a deep amber with dark undertones running through them. His left eyebrow had a small scar that cut through it. He looked to be about the same body type as Jasper too. He was wearing a black tee and ripped form-fitting jeans.

"Luca, there you are!" Zara came out of the kitchen cheerfully, she had an apron on. She must have been cooking and heard Luca come in. "We have company." She smiled and gestured at Jasper.

"Well, I figured that much." He teased Zara. "Did I forget about a meeting or event? Where is Kato?" Luca looked around the room.

"Actually," Zara's smile faded away. "Jasper is going to be staying with us for a little while."

"Oh," Luca's posture changed, "uh, okay. Where will he be sleeping?"

"Well," Zara fidgeted with her apron a little as she replied, "I was hoping you would allow Jasper to bunk with you until I can clean an area out for him." She looked up at Luca, "Would you be able to do that for me?"

"I guess." Luca looked at Jasper then at his mother and let out a sigh. "Is there really an option to say no?"

"Thanks, sweetie." She walked over and gave him a hug. "Jasper, that is okay with you, right? I'm sorry, but with short notice, I wasn't all that prepared for a guest."

"Uh, no, it's fine." Jasper looked at Zara and Luca, "As long as it's really okay with Luca? I don't want to intrude. I mean, I can sleep on the couch if it's an issue."

"Well," Luca sharply turned his head to his mom with a grin, "there's an option." He shrugged.

"Luca!" she gasped, swatting her hand at him.

"I'm kidding." They both began laughing. He turned

and looked at Jasper, "Just give me a bit to go clean it up, okay? Don't need to scare you away from our house on the first day now, do we?"

Jasper nodded his head and waved his hand, as to say no problem. Luca turned and ran upstairs to begin cleaning. Zara, satisfied with the arrangement, returned to the kitchen to finish cooking. Jasper followed behind her shortly after.

"Do you need any help in here?" he asked.

"Sure, sweetie. You could set the table for me. That would help a lot. Plates are in the cabinet, and silverware are in the drawer over there." She pointed as she talked, showing him where to look.

"So," Jasper grabbed everything, "do you guys not use your powers that much when you're away from Lyteshaed?" He asked as he worked.

"Honestly, we used to all the time." Zara looked up at Jasper, she was still worried about how he was doing but was also happy to see he was attempting to take part in his temporary environment, "Then we gradually drifted away from it. Sometimes it's nice to enjoy the small things. Yeah, sure, I could conjure up a delicious meal in a snap. But there's just something about learning the skill yourself and being proud of your effort. You know?" she turned back and started cooking. "Now that's not to say we don't use our powers, because we do." She walked away from the pot she was working on, the spoon continued stirring as she worked on another dish.

"I never stopped to look at it like that." Jasper smiled.

"I like it."

"Rooms done." Luca walked into the kitchen. "After we eat, I'll take you up."

"Sounds good." Jasper replied, he was done setting the table. "Zara, was there anything else you needed help with?"

"No, I'm about done here. You and Luca can go ahead and make your drinks and sit down." She turned the stove off and finished preparing the food.

"Here," Luca headed towards the cabinets, "You go ahead, I'll make our drinks." He said to Jasper. He made three drinks then sat them at the table. After that, he walked over to Zara, "Here, mom, you go sit. I'll make the plates."

"Well, aren't you being nice today." Zara looked at Luca lovingly, "Thanks, sweetie." Then she took off her apron, washed her hands, and walked over to the table to sit with Jasper.

Luca began making the plates. Zara had made spaghetti and meatballs, with some garlic cheese bread to go on the side. Jasper sat there, watching them both. Zara had been so kind during this transition. She made it easier than Jasper had thought it would be. He was very thankful. He had known both Zara and Luca since he was little, but only as fellow clan members. It was nice to see what they were like away from the clan. Jasper smiled.

"So, how was your day?" Zara asked Luca.

"Pretty peaceful, actually. I went for a walk on the trail in our woods, did some practicing, and went through some books." He replied. "How was your day?"

"Well," Zara looked at Jasper, "I had meetings to take care of. Lots of boring stuff." She continued eating.

"I get it, not my business." Luca smiled, but Jasper could tell he wanted to know what was up.

"It's nothing against you." Jasper spoke up, he knew what it was like to feel left out, "I asked her not to say anything. I'm still processing everything."

"I get it." Luca smiled again, but this one was real.

"Maybe you two can go out and get to know each other more tomorrow?" Zara spoke up.

"Mom," Luca coughed, "that was a bit forced, don't you think?"

"It's okay." Jasper laughed, "My dad would be the same way. Honestly, it would be nice to have someone to hang with and get my mind off of everything."

"Oh, okay. Sure." Luca replied.

They continued chatting and eating supper. When Jasper was finished eating, he inspected the table closer. He could not make out what the etchings were supposed to be, or if they even had a purpose.

"Zara?" Jasper looked up at her as he traced his finger against the design.

"Yes?" She answered.

"I was wondering what these etchings are here for?" He asked, looking back down at the table.

"Oh." Zara perked up, "That was a craft of mine and Luca's. Isn't that right?" She proudly looked at Luca.

"Yeah." Luca replied, less peppy than Zara, "We like to take things and put our own touch on them. Do you like it?" He asked.

"I do." Jasper nodded, "It's stunning, you guys did a really good job on it."

Once Luca and Zara were finished eating too, Jasper offered to help clean the dishes. Zara, however, refused the help and instead sent him with Luca to take his stuff to Luca's room and get settled in.

Luca's room was much smaller than Jasper's, but it was still a decent size. The theme of the house continued into it. His outer wall contained a window seat, full of pillows tucked against it. The top of the windows were crescent-shaped and stained glass, while the bottoms were clear. His bed was pretty big too. The headboard was wooden and had designs carved into it. There were short bedposts at the foot of the bed also. The floor was a dark, thick carpet. The walls were a light beige color. He had a couple of paintings and decorations hanging on the walls too.

"Nice room." Jasper turned to look at Luca, who had already begun changing his clothes.

"Thanks." Luca pulled his shorts up. "It does the job." He turned around shirtless and looked at Jasper. "Oh, I'm sorry. I didn't mean to make you uncomfortable. It's a habit."

"No," Jasper shook his head, "you're fine." He looked around for a place to set his stuff to keep up the act.

"Good." Luca laughed and walked over to his bed, "Looks like we are roommates until mom gets you a place cleaned out." He sat down on his bed and looked at Jasper, "You're not one of those birthday suit sleepers, right? No judgment, but if so, you need to grab an extra blanket." He pointed at the closet, "Because I'm a cuddler." He smirked, then began laughing. "No, I'm just messing with you, man." He laid down, climbing under the covers, "About the cuddling that is. I was serious about the extra cover." He laughed.

"You're good," Jasper chuckled. Luca seemed funny, they would both get along. "I sleep in shorts and a shirt. Speaking of, where's the bathroom."

"Oh, you're a shy one?" Luca grinned, "It's down the hall to the left."

Jasper nodded then headed to the bathroom to change. He didn't bring clothes so he would have to do like when he was at the beach. He took his clothes off and set them to the side. Then, with a graceful sweep of his hand, Jasper conjured his clothes for the night. As his hand glided up his body, a pair of silk shorts and a loose shirt appeared on him. He looked in the mirror and fixed his clothes. He would have to transport more of his clothes here to-morrow when he knew where he could store them. Jasper headed back to Luca's room. While his head pounded, and his heart was heavy, he was relieved his transition had gone so smoothly.

When Jasper walked into the room, the lights were off. There were glowing stones stashed in random places all over. They reflected illusions of the night sky all over the walls and ceiling. It was astonishing and peaceful all at once. Luca was already asleep. Jasper walked over to the other side of the bed and got in. He laid on his back, staring up at the imitated night sky. Eventually, his eyes became too heavy, and he drifted off into a deep sleep.

CHAPTER SEVEN

Jasper slept through the night, no nightmares, no visions, just a night of peacefulness. As he woke up, he stretched his arms out, for a moment he allowed himself to think the other day was just a dream. That he was still at home and in his bed, about to go meet his dad and Axton in the dining hall to get some breakfast. Of course, it all came flooding back to him when his hand grabbed Luca. Jasper jumped up.

"Woah, buy me a drink first." Luca laughed as he stretched, waking up too.

"Sorry." Jasper began to get out of bed.

"You're fine." Luca shrugged it off and continued laying down. "Oh, by the way, I cleaned out some drawers in my dresser for you. There's also some space for you to hang stuff if you need to. Mom means well, but it'll probably be a while before she actually gets to clean you out an area." Luca gave up on the thought of him being able to go back to sleep and began to sit up. "The stuff on the right is mine. The area on the left is where you can put your things." He pointed to his closet.

Jasper walked over and waved his hand over his half of the closet. He did the same to each empty drawer in the dresser. As he did this, his clothes appeared and filled the emptiness. While it wasn't home, now he had something to make it feel more like it for a while.

"You're way better at that than I am." Luca said as he walked over to examine the now full closet.

"It just takes some practice. You'll get the hang of it." Jasper encouraged, but he couldn't help but wonder if Luca was just trying to be polite.

"Well, go ahead and get dressed. Mom likes to have breakfast before she leaves. It's a thing we do." Luca started changing into his clothes for the day.

Jasper picked out an outfit and did the same. He caught Luca staring at him, chuckling, out of the corner of his eye.

"What?" Jasper asked.

"Nothing." Luca chuckled more, "I guess you're not as shy as I thought you were."

"Well, I guess there are lots of things you don't know about me." Jasper smirked.

Once they finished changing, Jasper and Luca headed down to meet Zara in the kitchen. As they got closer, they could hear items clattering. Jasper could smell cinnamon and maple syrup. He wondered what they were going to walk into her making.

"Good morning, boys. How'd you sleep?" Zara asked as the boys entered the kitchen.

"Good." They both replied.

"What's for breakfast?" Luca asked as he took a seat at the table.

"French toast." Zara turned around with a plate full of food and carried it to the table. "Jasper, sweetie, can you grab the maple syrup? It's right there on the counter." She pointed toward the counter with her head as she set the plate down.

Jasper grabbed the syrup and joined them at the table. While he did miss his dad and Axton, it was nice to have something similar to his morning routine with Zara and Luca. He and his father did the same thing to start their day. It was their way of putting in the effort to involve each other in their lives.

"So, what are you boys planning on doing for the day?" Zara asked.

"Probably just showing Jasper around?" Luca looked at Jasper, then Zara.

"It'll be nice to get away and clear my mind. What about you?" Jasper asked Zara.

"I have a meeting with the Elders, we have much to discuss." Zara responded.

They chatted through the rest of breakfast. When they were finished, they all got ready to go their separate ways for the day. Zara headed out before the boys did. She told them she would be home late. Jasper half wanted to go with her to be a part of the meeting, but he knew he also needed to take a break from everything. He was missing the ocean right about now.

"You ready to head out?" Luca approached Jasper.

"Actually," Jasper responded, "what do you think about changing up our plans?"

"What do you have in mind?" Luca's interest was piqued.

"How about we go to the beach? I could really use a beach day." Jasper said, wondering if Luca would go for it.

"I'd love a beach day," Luca paused and laughed, "but we are nowhere near the ocean."

"Well," Jasper looked down nervously then back at Luca, "I actually have that part figured out. I know the sigil the Chancellor and the Elders use to go wherever they want."

"What? How?" Luca thought for a moment, connecting the dots as he grinned, "Oh, you're so lucky! That could come in very handy."

"I can share it with you. If you keep it a secret between us." Jasper bargained.

Luca grinned and nodded, "One issue, though." He gestured at his clothes, "I don't have swim clothes."

"You can borrow mine." Jasper gestured for Luca to follow him upstairs.

After changing and getting together what they would need to have a fun day out, Jasper began working on the sigil. He used Luca's bedroom door as the portal way. Now he had to choose a destination. He wanted to use the shop but did not think that was the best idea when trying to sneak away for the day. He eventually decided on the bathroom where he usually changes at.

"How will we know that no one is in the bathroom when we go through?" Luca asked, "I'm all for sneaking off, but I don't want to risk exposure."

Jasper stood there for a moment, he agreed with Luca. There had to be a way to ensure the other end of the portal was empty. Then something came to Jasper. Before he knew it, he was drawing a weird symbol in the air over the portal. Once he was done, he took a step back. Luca and Jasper looked at one another, neither was sure what just happened. They looked back at the floating blue sigil, it was made out of Jasper's energy.

"How did you do that?" Luca gasped.

"I, I don't know." Jasper stumbled.

"What now?" Luca asked.

Jasper walked back up to the sigil and pushed it towards the portal. It absorbed the sigil and began to glow brighter until it was clear. Jasper and Luca were now looking through the portal.

"How is this happening?" Luca turned and asked Jasper.

"It just came to me." Jasper shrugged, "I don't even know what it means, or that I could even do it again if I wanted to."

They turned and faced the portal again. People were

walking in and out of the bathroom, but no one noticed them standing there watching them. Whatever was allowing them to peak through was one-sided. They stood there waiting for it to empty out and become safe for them to walk through.

"Okay, you ready?" Jasper looked a Luca, who nodded back at him. Then they both stepped through.

They entered into the empty bathroom. Jasper was still trying to figure out where the sigil he drew came from, and how he was able to channel his energy to draw it in midair. He looked over at Luca, who seemed to be going through the same thoughts in his head. Luca turned and saw Jasper looking at him.

"Let's forget that just happened and talk about it later." He tried to ease Jasper, "We're here to enjoy the water and sand, right?"

"Yeah," Jasper shook the thoughts out of his mind, "you're right. Let's go."

They exited the bathroom and headed towards the beach. Jasper could tell Luca was excited to be at the beach, he wondered how often Luca got to go. Jasper couldn't ruin it for him by telling him the real reason they were there. He was hoping to see Freya. She had to know more about what was going on. It was no coincidence she showed up around the time of everything else falling apart.

Jasper led Luca to an empty spot to lay their stuff and sit down. Jasper drew the sigil he drew the last time he was at the beach. It would block out the noise, but also allow him and Luca to talk without eavesdroppers. Once he was finished, he threw out his towel over it and sat down.

"You know what people are thinking, right?" Luca began smiling as he threw his towel down and joined Jasper. "Two shirtless, good looking, guys sitting together on the beach?" he nudged Jasper. Luca was trying to lighten the mood. He could see something was on Jasper's mind.

"Oh, is that so?" Jasper nudged Luca back. "Well then," he jumped up, holding his hand out to help Luca up, "let's give them something to talk about."

Luca grabbed Jasper's hand, and Jasper pulled him up. They both started laughing and took off, running to the ocean. The cooling water, the warm sun, it all felt amazing. Jasper let everything drift away as he just enjoyed the moment. They swam, splashed, fought the waves, and hunted shells. After a while, they got worn out and walked back up to their spot. They both fell down on their towels out, of breath, laughing.

"Thanks, Luca." Jasper caught his breath. "Today was greatly needed. Thanks for spending it with me."

"No problem. Thanks for inviting me." Luca said.

"Can I tell you something?" Jasper got serious, and his more vulnerable side took over.

"Sure, what's up?" Luca rolled over, off his back and onto his stomach, facing Jasper.

"I'm not sure I am ready to handle everything that's in store for me. Everyone is being so supportive of it all, but I'm just not sure. In a day, I went from what I thought was an average and happy life, to having my whole world blown up in front of me."

Luca stared at Jasper for a moment, "I didn't know you were dealing with all of that. I'm sorry."

"No, you're good." Jasper rolled over onto his stomach, "I was the one who asked your mom not to mention anything. I guess I thought if I didn't talk about it, I could ignore it."

"I get it." Luca paused for a moment, wondering if he could ask what he wanted, "If I can ask, what exactly is going on? My mom's been different since you both got here."

Jasper knew he owed it to Luca to fill him in on what was going on. It was not only fair, but it was also the right thing to do. After all, he was living with Luca and Zara for now. Any moment there could be an attack and Luca should be adequately prepared. Jasper sat up and gestured for Luca to do the same. What better time to fill him in than now?

"Where should I even begin?" Jasper sighed.

"Hey!" a female voice called, "Jasper, right?"

Jasper knew that voice. It was Freya. He turned his head all around, scanning the beach for her. Luca did the same.

"Where is that voice coming from?" Luca continued scanning the beach.

"It's Freya." Jasper continued searching.

"Who's Freya?" Luca questioned.

"That would be me." Freya walked up to the boys, smiling, holding out her hand to shake Luca's. For a moment, her facial expression changed, but only for a moment. Then she turned, going back to smiling, and greeted Jasper. "How are you?"

"Jasper," Luca looked at him, confused, "who is this?"

"Freya. I met her the other day on the beach." Jasper replied, not taking his eyes off of Freya, who continued smiling.

"Oh, I'm sorry. Am I interrupting something?" Freya took a step back, placing her hand on her chest while staring at both boys.

Luca began to speak but was cut off by Jasper, "No, we're just visiting the beach for the day. Join us?"

Freya nodded and sat down in between the boys. Luca sat at one end, confused. One moment he and Jasper were talking, he was finally going to be told what was happening. Then this mystery girl comes along, and Jasper changed. Why?

Jasper, on the other side, sat facing Freya. He had so many questions he wanted, and needed, to ask. Where to begin? Would she even answer them?

"Freya?" Jasper started, "The other day you said I was someone like you. What did you mean by that?"

"Oh," Freya smiled, "you've found something out. Haven't you? I can see it in your eyes."

"That's a bit of an understatement." Jasper nodded.

"I'm sure it's a lot to take in." Freya sympathized, "I'm actually curious as to how something like this was able to be kept hidden so well from you."

"I'm just coming to find out how myself." Jasper replied.

"Yeah, but didn't you notice that you could do things that the others could not?" Freya asked.

"No," Jasper shook his head, "I've never done anything that no one else couldn't." He shot a glance at Luca. He wanted to tell Freya about the sigil, but he had to make sure she was telling the truth before he even thought about trusting her.

"Really? Wow! Whoever hid you must've been very powerful to be able to also hide your talents from you." Freya was surprised, and intrigued, by what Jasper was saying.

"How do you know I was hidden?" Jasper, growing suspicious, asked.

"Well, that's the only rational explanation." She turned and looked at Luca for the first time since the conversations started, "Right?"

Luca nodded, but didn't respond. He was still taking everything in. He wondered if this stranger could actually be trusted. She didn't seem harmful, but looks could be misleading.

"Here," She stood up, "let me show you."

Freya walked off to the water and searched the sand. Jasper and Luca stayed sitting on their towels, both not knowing what to think about what was going on. Freya came walking back to the boys, but she had something in her hands. As she got closer, she kneeled in the sand and showed them what she was holding. It was a dead crab. It must have been crushed by a passerby or something.

"What are you going to do with that?" Luca asked, slightly disgusted.

"Just watch." Freya grinned and closed her hands. Pink energy swirled inside her hands. The boys could see flashes of color through the spaces in her hands cupped together. Freya closed her eyes and started whispering some chant, but Jasper couldn't make it out. Then she opened her hands.

"Wow!" Jasper jumped back, "How did you?"

The crab stood and then climbed out of Freya's hand. She had brought it back to life. But no one could do that. It had been attempted by many powerful beings, but no one had ever been strong enough to break death's hold. Yet, here sat Freya. This small, young girl had done it.

"Can I do that?" Jasper was amazed.

"I don't know." Freya shrugged her shoulders, "We all have something that we can do. Some of us have many talents. Some of us have only a few, or even only one. For right now, that's the extent of mine. I can only do small creatures like that crab, and even that drains me big time."

"I have so many questions." Jasper sat up, scooting closer to Freya.

"I'm sure you do." She smiled, but Jasper could tell something was up.

"Are you okay?" He asked.

"I just need to go and rest." She nodded slowly, "Like I

said, it takes a lot out of me." She began standing up.

"Wait." Jasper held out his hand.

"Jasper," Luca blocked him, "She's weak. She needs to go."

"But I have so much that I need to know." Jasper said, looking at Luca and then at Freya.

"He's right, Jasper." Freya was not as bubbly as Jasper had come to see. She was drained. "I overdid it. I should go."

"Okay." Jasper wanted to keep asking, but he knew he needed to let her go. "At least tell me how I can get in touch with you." Jasper pleaded.

Freya turned and faced Jasper. She reached out her hand to him. As he reached out his, she flipped her hand over, revealing a blank piece of paper. Jasper reached out and grabbed it.

"If you need me, write my name on this paper with a location and time to meet. Then charge it with your energy and burn it. It will come to me, and I will meet you." Then she walked away.

Jasper and Luca looked at the paper. Jasper had read about a paper like this. It was what clans used to communicate before phones, and other technological advances, were made by society.

"Couldn't she have just given you her phone number?" Luca finally spoke up.

Jasper just stopped, looked at him, and shook his head with a grin. He got up, grabbed his towel, and kicked sand over the sigil to deactivate it.

"What? It would have been much easier." Luca laughed as he grabbed his stuff and followed Jasper.

The boys stood outside the bathroom, waiting for the coast to be clear. Once it was safe, they walked in, and Jasper got to work on the portal. He set it to take them to Luca's room.

"Ready?" He asked Luca.

"Let's go." Luca said as he stepped through the portal.

Jasper took a breath. He looked down at the paper, then folded it up and placed it in his pocket. He stepped through the portal following Luca. When he stepped into the room, he saw Luca staring at him. No, he wasn't staring at him, he was staring behind him.

"What are you looking at?" He asked, concerned.

Zara cleared her throat as she tapped Jasper on the shoulder. Jasper froze. Then he turned around to face Zara, who stood sternly outside the doorway with her arms folded across her chest.

"Oh."

CHAPTER EIGHT

"So…" Zara stepped into Luca's room, "Are you boys going to tell me where you went today?"

She was not happy. Jasper stood there, wondering if he should tell her everything, or wait until he knew more himself. She could clearly see they were still in their swimwear. There was no hiding they went somewhere with water. Jasper began to speak up but was cut off.

"Don't be mad at him mom." Luca stepped forward, "It was my idea. I wanted to go to the beach. I figured he had to have seen the sigil you used to get here. So, I assumed he would be able to get us there."

"Luca." Zara shook her head and looked down, "I don't know what to say about this."

"I just thought it was something that we could do that was fun. Besides, it let him escape from whatever is going on, that neither of you will tell me about." Luca looked back and forth at Zara and Jasper.

Jasper stood there, confused. Why was Luca taking the fall for him? Why was he not telling Zara what he had witnessed him do? Jasper could also see that Luca was quickly becoming hurt over not being filled in on what was going on.

"That does not excuse anything." Zara raised her head and looked at Luca. "You both broke some rules by doing this, and you put us all at risk." She looked at Jasper, "You're lucky it was Victor that spotted you, and that he came to me instead of going to your dad."

"I'm sorry, Zara." Jasper said as he looked down.

"You know what's going on. You've got to stay safe. Pulling stunts like this is not going to cut it." She sighed, "You both need to shower and clean up this sand while you're at it." She motioned to the floor, "We will talk more in the morning. There's food in the fridge to warm up if you're still hungry." She shook her head and then walked out of the room, closing the door behind her.

Luca grabbed some clothes and went to the bathroom to shower and clean up. Jasper stood alone in the room, going over what just happened. He felt terrible for stressing Zara out, and he should have thought about the consequences his choice would have. He was also still wondering why Luca had taken the fall for him. Luca could have easily told her it was Jasper's idea to go, about the sigil, and about Freya. Yet, he didn't. Why?

When Luca came back into the room, he remained quiet. Jasper grabbed his clothes, took the paper out of his pocket, placed it in a drawer, then went and took a shower too. The more he thought about it, the more he began thinking Luca could be someone he could trust during all of this. He needed someone he could trust. It was settled. When he was done showering, Jasper was going to go back in the room and tell Luca everything. He finished and headed back to talk to Luca.

"Luca?" Jasper cautiously entered the room, attempting to sense Luca's mood.

"Yeah." Luca replied, sitting on his bed.

"Thanks." Jasper said as he walked over to join him.

"Don't mention it." Luca shifted away from Jasper.

"No, I mean it." Jasper could tell Luca was holding something back, "Thanks. You didn't have to do that, but you did."

"You're right," Luca turned and faced Jasper, "I didn't have to. I don't know why I did. I'm the one being left in the dark."

"That's what I want to talk to you about." Jasper sympathized, "I want to fill you in on everything. I would like for us to be friends and to be able to trust one another. For that to happen, you need to be fully prepared for what is coming."

They both situated themselves better to be comfortable. Then Jasper told Luca everything. He started with the ritual. He even told Luca about how he could hear the ancestors. Jasper told him about the vision and The Lady in White. He told Luca how he was told about his birth parents and showed him the box, journal, and necklace. Jasper also told Luca how he was now the only one who was completely filled in. Jasper had told Luca things that he hadn't even told Kato or Zara.

"This is a lot to take in." Luca finished reading the journal and placed it back into the box.

"I'm trusting you with all of this." Jasper said as he closed the box, and it sealed itself shut.

"Don't worry, you can trust me." Luca promised, "I've got your back."

"It's nice to have someone to talk to about all of this, and to not have to stress about hiding anything." Jasper said, feeling relieved for the first time since everything began.

"I can imagine. So, then what is up with this Freya chick?" Luca asked.

"I honestly don't know," Jasper shrugged, "She appeared after I had the vision and was talking about how we were alike. Before I could ask anything, Victor showed up and told me my dad had sent for me."

"We need to find out what all she knows." Luca said.

"I agree. I think I'm going to set up a meeting with her soon using that paper." Jasper said, pointing to the dresser where he stored it.

"It sounds like we need to have some training sessions. If we are about to have a battle, we need to be prepared for it." Luca's stomach gurgled, "It also sounds like my

stomach thinks we need to go down and raid the fridge."
He laughed.

"Mine concurs with that assessment." Jasper chuckled.

The boys went downstairs and heated up some of the leftovers Zara had made. They sat at the table laughing about their day. They also discussed Freya bringing the crab back to life. Luca thanked Jasper for taking him to the beach. Even though it ended with him most likely getting some kind of punishment, it was worth the experience. When they were done eating, they headed back up to Luca's room.

"So tomorrow," Jasper went to his side of the bed, "I guess we can go ahead and talk to your mom about some type of advanced training?"

"I think, for now, the best thing we can do is get some rest. That way, we are prepared for the speech she is going to give us both in the morning." Luca climbed into bed.

Jasper laid down and began thinking. They would need to have some training to prepare for the fight ahead of them. Everyone in Lyteshaed is trained in basic battle techniques, but there hasn't been a battle in so long. They would need more advanced and real-world training. The basics would not have them prepared for what he had foreseen. He tried to let his thoughts fade away as he turned off the light. There would be time to discuss and prepare later. For now, Luca was right. They needed their rest.

Jasper looked around. He was back in the field where he last saw The Lady in White. What was he doing back here?

How did he get here? He looked around but couldn't see anyone. Then a ray of moonlight came down from the sky, touching the ground.

"Hello?" Jasper said as he looked into the light to see if he could see anyone.

"Jasper." A familiar voice spoke from within the light.

The Lady in White then stepped out of the light. She looked the same as she did last time, except her eyes were now brown and no longer reflected her silver energy out of them.

"We meet again." She greeted him as she walked up to Jasper.

"What is the purpose of all of this?" Jasper had many questions to ask.

"All in good time." She smiled.

"Can you at least tell me your name?" Jasper asked, "The Lady in White is a bit of a mouthful."

"Luna." She replied.

"Luna, what can you tell me about my parents?" Jasper wondered if they were even still alive.

"Your parents love you. What they did was for the protection of you." Luna explained.

"What did they need to protect me from?" Jasper questioned.

"There are forces that would not want you to reunite with your parents. They had to put a plan in action to ensure your survival." Luna warned.

"That still doesn't fully answer the question." Jasper

sighed, he knew enough to know he was not going to get the full answer right now, "Can you at least tell me if they are still alive?"

"I cannot answer that factually. Whatever they did to hide you, hid their identities from me. I can only tell you what I feel, and that is that they are both still safe. Yet, I fear for them too." Her expression changed to a remorseful one, "I wish I knew more, but my knowledge of this situation is hindered. I do know that the more you discover through the journal, the more my memory comes back."

"What do you mean?" Jasper asked.

"Once you read from the journal, a sigil came to me. I remember being told to give it to you, that it would reveal more of the journal to you. I also remember that the person who told me this was someone I trusted undeniably." Her expression was back to a smile, and she seemed hopeful again. Then she extended her hand and held out a piece of paper with a sigil on it. "Draw this in the journal your mother left you, and it will reveal more." She withdrew her hand.

"Can you tell me anything else?" Jasper wanted to know anything he could.

"You are about to go through many trials that will test you in different ways. Do not give in. Do not give up. Trust yourself, and you will find the answers to all of your questions." She began walking back to the light.

"Wait!" Jasper followed her but was too late. She was already inside the light again. He tried, but something was blocking him from being able to enter into it himself.

"We will meet again." Her voice echoed as the light faded away.

Jasper woke up and sat up in bed. He wondered if what just happened was real or a dream. Then he looked down in his hand and saw a piece of paper. He flipped it over. It was the one she gave him. So, the dream was real.

"You okay?" Luca was standing in the closet, picking out clothes.

"I don't know." Jasper held the piece of paper up.

"Where'd you get that from?" Luca asked as he continued digging through his closet.

"Luna." Jasper stayed sitting in bed.

"Who's Luna?" Luca poked his head out of the closet.

"The Lady in White." Jasper answered.

Luca stopped digging through the closet and walked over to Jasper. He took the paper from him and examined it.

"What's this supposed to do?" he asked.

"It's supposed to reveal more of what my mother wrote to me in the journal." Jasper replied.

"Dude, you need to use it then. You need to know what she wrote to you." Luca got slightly more excited about the situation than he should have.

"I guess you're right." Jasper said as he got out of bed and walked to the box.

"Boys!" Zara shouted from downstairs, "If you're awake, I need you to come on down."

"Her hearing is bionic." Luca laughed as he began

walking to his door, "Let's go get this over with."

Jasper nodded as he slipped the piece of paper into the box. The journal would have to wait. He had to go deal with the repercussions of yesterday. They both walked downstairs to meet her. Both of them were hoping that she was going to let the situation go and move on, but they knew they couldn't be that lucky.

"Great, you're both up." Zara motioned for the boys to come into the living room, "Come sit down." She patted the couch.

The boys looked at one another. They were confused. Last night, she was very upset with them. They were sure she was going to be angry with them for a while, but she didn't seem to be mad anymore. She looked the complete opposite. They nodded at each other and walked to the couch and sat down.

"Is everything okay?" Jasper asked.

"Yes." Zara replied. "I've decided to let yesterday go. You're both not off the hook quite yet, but I will not continue with any lecture. I trust you both know what you did was wrong, and have learned from it. Yes?"

"Yes, but…" Jasper started to explain it was his idea but was cut off.

"No, no. It's done. We move on." She instructed.

Jasper and Luca looked at each other again. This was very odd, what happened for her to change her mind on the matter that fast?

"Mom, is everything okay?" Luca asked.

"Yes, or well, it will be." She replied, looking back and forth at both boys.

"Then what did you need to talk about?" Luca was still wary. Sometimes his mom would act really happy right before delivering some difficult news.

"Well," she looked down, then up at Jasper, "the other Elders and I have decided to pass on knowledge of advanced practices. You need to be well prepared for what is coming."

"It's okay, I've told Luca about everything. He knows what is going on." Jasper replied, "I actually wanted to talk to you about training. You're right, we all need to be prepared."

"Yes, *we* do." Zara looked at Jasper.

"What does that mean?" Luca spoke up, noticing the strange tone in her voice.

"Luca," she turned to face him, "I have talked to Kato. He has agreed to let you stay with him until all of this is taken care of. This is not something I want you to be a part of. I need to know that you are safe."

"What?" Luca was shocked.

"Zara, if this is about the beach. It was my idea, not his." Jasper interjected. He had just opened up to Luca about everything. He had someone he could trust, and now he was about to go back to being on his own. There had to be a way to get her to let Luca stay.

"No!" Zara sternly turned and looked at Jasper, her protective side coming out, "That's not what this is about.

This is about knowing my son is safe, along with the rest of the clan."

"Mom," Luca began, Zara turned to look at him, "Jasper has told me what he has seen. I know that you are trying to hide the fact that you are scared and worried, but I'm not running away."

"Luca…" Zara sighed.

"No, mom." He cut her off, "Jasper needs us. We need to stand by him, not run away." Luca looked at Jasper, then back at his mom, "He has trusted me with what is going on. I will not leave him to deal with it on his own. I'm staying."

"Luca…" Zara tried to speak again but again was interrupted.

"I'm staying, mom, and you won't change my mind." Luca stated firmly, but sympathetically, to his mom. He knew she was worried about him, but he also knew she knew he was right.

"Okay." Zara looked at both boys, "Okay. I'll inform Kato and the Elders of this. I will have to get approval for you too Luca. If we are going to do this, I need to know I can trust you boys. No more sneaking off. If you have to go somewhere, you tell me. The only way this works is if we are all on the same page. No secrets, agreed?"

"Agreed." Jasper and Luca nodded their heads.

"Good." Zara stood up, "Why did I have to raise such a brave child?" she shook her head, mumbling to herself as she turned and walked out of the room.

Luca and Jasper looked at each other. They agreed no more secrets, yet they were still keeping some.

"We will tell her about Freya, and everything else, eventually. Just not yet." Jasper spoke quietly, so Zara would not hear them talking.

"I agree, no reason to go to her with too many unknown variables." Luca quietly whispered back, "I think we should go see what more that sigil reveals in your journal."

Jasper nodded then got up from the couch. Jasper was happy to know that Luca was sticking with him and had his back. If everything was to be believed, he was in for quite the journey. It was nice to know he had someone he could trust.

"Let's go get this over with, I guess." Jasper said as he began heading upstairs.

"No time like the present." Luca sighed and got up from the couch, "Mom, we're headed to my room. Holler if you need anything." He shouted to Zara.

"Okay, I'm heading off to talk with everyone. We will begin planning when I get back." She replied, poking her head out of the doorway.

Luca nodded to her, then turned to follow Jasper.

"Hey, wait for me!" he shouted as he raced up the stairs.

CHAPTER NINE

Jasper sat on Luca's bed with the box on his lap. He took a breath as he opened it and pulled out the journal and piece of paper that The Lady in White, who he now knew was known as Luna, gave him in the dream.

"I can't believe she was able to give me something in a dream, and that I was able to bring it back with me." Jasper said as he closed the box and set it beside him.

"Here." Luca handed Jasper a pen so he could draw the sigil, "Whatever she is, she must be powerful. If you stop to think about it," he paused in awe, "that would mean you are too."

Jasper turned and looked at Luca. Somehow, Luca was able to take what was happening and try to put a positive spin on it. Jasper did not know how he was able to do it so easily. There was no way he could do something like that. Jasper was doing well enough to keep himself pulled together.

"I guess. Doesn't any of this freak you out?" Jasper asked.

"I mean, in a way, yeah. But I'm more intrigued by it all. Aren't you? We have a knowledge that many others on this planet do not. Are you really going to say you never wondered what else was out there?" Luca replied in an almost energetic state.

"I guess I have always been drawn to what is beyond us." Jasper looked back down at the journal, "I just never thought that I would be a part of it."

"Jasper," Luca put his arm around Jasper's shoulder, "you need to stop looking at this as a bad situation. You found out some messed up stuff, sure. But in the process, you've found out you are something more powerful than any of us could imagine. You've been given a gift, accept it, embrace it. The sooner you do, the sooner you'll begin healing."

"I know, you're right. I'm trying. It's just a lot." Jasper said as he opened the journal to the first empty page after what he had already read.

Jasper drew the sigil at the top of the page. When he was done, he sat back up and waited for something to happen.

"What now?" Luca asked

"I don't know, I guess we wait?" Jasper shrugged.

They waited and watched the journal. Then slowly, it began to soak up the sigil until it vanished into the journal.

After it was gone, ink began appearing. It was his mother's handwriting.

"It's another entry from my mom." Jasper stated.

"Well, what are you waiting for? Read it!" Luca nudged him, "I'll leave you to it." He got up and walked over to the nook in his wall and sat down.

Jasper watched as the ink continued writing. It was as if his mom was here with him now, writing the words for the first time. Once it was finished, he began reading.

My sweet Jasper,

> *So, you have seen The Lady in White again, and she gave you the sigil to reveal more. I am sure she filled you in on how her knowledge is tied to how much you reveal. I did that to ensure everyone's safety. If no one is able to remember you, or us, then they will not be able to hunt for you.*

> *Jasper, that means your father and I will have to forget you too. I am only allowing those who need to know to be able to remember certain essential information. However, as you continue to chisel away through this journal their memories of everything will come back too.*

> *I must warn you, that means those who want to hurt us and keep us apart will begin remembering too. Chances are, they have already started to sense something unraveling. You need to be careful and aware of those around you and your surroundings.*

> *There is more I must tell you too. What I did to*

everyone, also had an effect on you. I locked your abilities. You will be able to do as others, maybe better, but never able to do more. You will start to, if you have not already, notice odd things happening. Things you used to not be able to do, or never thought possible, you will start being capable of.

You need to begin working on what you can. You need to strengthen yourself to be prepared for anything. Start by channeling your energy outside of your body. You know how to do this on small scales through the clan. We can do what they have taught, but on a much larger scale. You can bring your energy around your body, expand it, and shape it. The only limitation is your belief in what you can do. Once you can bring it out, keep going at it. You need to be able to do this without thinking about it. You will be drained when you start, but fight through. You have no idea what you are capable of.

One last thing before I end this entry. You will need to find something. The necklace that I left in the box, I am sure you have noticed the hole in it. It needs to be put back together. Why is not important right now. To find the first piece, you need to get Axton to remember the instructions I gave him. I cannot tell you how to get him to remember, you need to be able to discover it on your own. Trust your abilities. If you do that, then it will come to you. He will tell you what to do from there.

My baby, I am so very proud of you. I cannot wait until the day we are all together again.

"So?" Luca walked back over to Jasper, seeing that he was finished reading.

"Here." Jasper handed him the journal.

Jasper sat there, watching as Luca read through what he just had. He watched as the expressions changed on Luca's face. Jasper went through everything in his head.

"Wow." Luca closed the journal.

"Yeah." Jasper replied.

"Well, at least we know what that whole sigil thing was. You need to start practicing, I wonder what else you can do." Luca was back to being excited about it all.

"What about the Axton part?" Jasper asked Luca, trying to talk through what he just read.

"Well, again, sounds like you need to practice. The sigil you did to glimpse through the portal was an accident. You need to be able to control yourself better to figure out what Axton knows. Once you do," Luca smiled, "sounds like we have a journey ahead of us."

"We?" Jasper was still surprised none of this made Luca shy away.

"Yeah, we. You think I'm not going to see how this all ends? I'm in this for the long-haul." Luca replied, getting up from the bed.

"I don't want to tell your mom everything just yet." Jasper looked at Luca, "We can tell her about more being revealed in the journal and me being told to practice my energy work. I don't want to drag Axton into this until I know how to make him remember."

"And, Freya?" Luca asked, "What about her? Can we trust her?"

"She's the only other person like me. What other choice do I have?" Jasper got up and walked over to the dresser where the paper was stored to call for Freya, "I think after we tell your mom, we need to tell her about Freya too. We need to see if she knows anything. My mom said that others would have their memories restored. Maybe Freya is one of them who will remember more too?"

"If it's what you think we should do, then I can't stop you. I think you should be careful with what you tell her, though. At least until you know you can trust her completely." Luca's attitude was more cautious.

Jasper noticed Luca's posture changed with the mention of Freya, but didn't understand why. For him to be so interested in all of this, Jasper would have thought he would want to dissect Freya's knowledge of everything. Maybe Luca was just being protective. Jasper shrugged it off and nodded in agreement. He would only tell Freya what she needed to know and find out what she knew. Maybe she could help him learn how to manipulate his energy the way his mother mentioned.

"Boys, I'm back!" Zara called out.

"We'll be right down!" Luca called back to her. "Come on, let's go fill her in." Then he turned and headed on downstairs, as Jasper followed behind.

"How did it go?" Luca asked as he walked downstairs.

"It took some skill and persuasion, but I got the others to approve for you to be trained also." Zara proudly replied. "We can't waste any time. We need to begin your training now."

"Actually," Jasper stopped her, "we need to talk to you about something."

"Yes?" Zara stopped and turned around. She noticed the look on Jasper's face was serious, "Here, why don't we go sit in the living room. You can tell me whatever is on your mind."

They all walked into the living room and sat down. Jasper had to be careful about what he told her. There were still things that he wanted to keep private for just a little bit longer. At least until he could make better sense out of it himself.

"I was visited by The Lady in White." Jasper began.

"When?" Zara was shocked.

"Last night, in a dream." Jasper explained.

"Why am I just now hearing about this?" Zara scolded.

Jasper figured she would be upset when he told her about his dream. After all, they had just promised her no more secrets, and here they were basically telling her they lied when they accepted the deal with her.

"You had so much on your plate already mom. He didn't want to bother you with information if it ended up being a dead end." Luca interjected.

"That may be, but from now on I want to know when you hear from her." Zara nodded but was clearly upset with this delay in information. "What did she say?"

"She gave me a sigil to draw in my journal. She told me it would reveal more information to me." Jasper said, handing her the paper with the sigil on it.

"And?" she asked, handing the paper back to Jasper.

"It revealed another entry from my mom. She gave me more information about what is going on and what she did. I was told to begin training my abilities. That as I reveal more, I will unlock more of my true potential. For now, I am supposed to begin by working on manipulating my energy." Jasper replied.

"What does that mean?" Zara asked.

"Well, for example, when we used the portal to go to the beach. I was able to draw a sigil in mid-air with my energy." Jasper began to explain but was cut off.

"What? How is that possible?" Zara was shocked.

"I'm still not entirely sure, but it allowed us to peek through the portal without being seen to make sure the coast was clear." Jasper continued, "Apparently, I can send my energy out of my body and manipulate it in many possible ways."

"It's actually really cool to see him do it, mom." Luca expressed, trying to keep his mom from freaking out.

"This is new for sure. We will have to figure out a way to safely let you train this ability. There is no knowledge of anyone being able to do something like you are explaining." Zara replied after composing herself back to a calmer state.

"Well," Jasper looked down then back up at Zara, "I

actually know someone that may be able to help."

"What? Who?" Zara was confused.

"Her name is Freya. I met her at the beach. She claims to be like me. We saw her do something that no one has ever been able to do before. Something we thought was not able to even be done." Jasper explained. "She brought a dead crab back to life."

"How can that be?" Zara gasped.

"It took a lot out of her, but she gave me a paper to use to be able to contact her." Jasper took the paper out of his pocket, "With your permission, I want to invite her here to see what she can tell me. Maybe she can help me with training and figuring out what I am capable of."

Jasper watched as Zara took everything in that she was just told. She got up from the couch and paced the room, she was thinking. Jasper looked at Luca, who nodded back to him. After a moment, Zara rejoined them on the couch.

"I do not appreciate being in the dark, but I can tell this is sure to be a theme." She looked at both boys, realizing that Luca had been aware of this way before herself, "I at least need your word that I am notified of things as they become important and relevant. We must work together."

Jasper and Luca both nodded to her in agreement. They no longer had to feel bad about keeping secrets. They never planned to not tell her. They just wanted to be well informed before they ran to her and filled her in.

"As for Freya, I will allow it. But," she paused, "the house will need to be protected before any training happens. We do not need to alert anyone of power spikes." She looked at Luca, "I will need to get you a list of items to collect to do this." Then she looked at Jasper, "Go ahead and invite her here. I will arrange the basement for everyone to be able to train."

The boys nodded. They all got up from the couch, each of them knowing their task at hand. Luca and Zara walked down to the basement. Luca would collect the supplies needed to protect and shield the house, while Zara rearranged everything.

Jasper began writing on the paper to call for Freya. He wrote her name, the address, and time to meet as she had instructed. Then he charged the paper with his energy and lit a match to burn it. He stood watching as the paper burned brightly. The ashes of the paper began to rise into the air and then flashed away. Now all he could do was wait. He threw the match away and headed down to the basement to see if he could help out while they waited for Freya to arrive.

CHAPTER TEN

As they were finishing setting things up, they heard a knock from upstairs. They all looked at one another. It must be time for Freya to arrive.

"I'll go let her in" Jasper emptied his hands and headed upstairs.

Jasper walked towards the front door. As he did, the knocking began again. This time though, it sounded rushed, panicked almost. He wondered why she would knock like that.

"Come on in." Jasper said as he opened the door. Then he saw her. "Whoa, Freya, what happened?" He pulled her into the house.

Freya did not look good, and she seemed frightened. Her clothes were torn, her hair was all messed up, and she had streaks down her face like she had just been crying.

"Zara!" Jasper called out. He didn't know what to do

for Freya.

"Jasper, what's the... Oh dear!" she rushed over to Freya and Jasper.

Freya grabbed Jasper as she began crying. Jasper and Zara looked at one another. He didn't know what to do. Jasper hugged her back.

"Here, you guys go sit on the couch." Zara pointed, "I'll go get Luca. We will grab some things for you to clean up and get you out of these dirty clothes." She tried to hide her worry as she rushed off to the basement.

"Freya?" Jasper got Freya settled on the couch, "What happened to you?"

"It was Camille." Freya was trying to pull herself together.

"Who's Camille?" Jasper asked, confused.

"She's like us. She's not from here." Freya began.

"You mean there are more people like us here?" Jasper was shocked, "Wait! Why did she do this to you?"

"She's not a good person. Not everyone like us is. Some are purely evil. They travel to other worlds spreading their influence." She replied, but her panic was beginning to come back.

"Calm down, you're fine." Jasper grabbed her and hugged her, "You're safe now. I'm sure Zara will let you stay with us until we get all of this figured out."

Freya pulled her head back and looked at Jasper, they both locked eyes.

"Thank you, Jasper. I don't know what I would have done if you didn't reach out to me." She began to lean towards him.

At first, Jasper froze, causing Freya to pull back. She sunk back into the couch as she began apologizing. Jasper sat there quietly, processing what just happened. Sure, he liked her but was it the right time for something like this? He watched as her eyes began to water. He saw how uncomfortable he had made her. Jasper reached his hand out setting it on Freya's to calm her down. He felt her pulse racing, her hand shaking. She looked at him remorsefully. She began to speak, but stopped. Jasper reached his other hand out, fixing a fallen strand of hair and pushing it behind her ear. She reached her hand up and held his. They locked eyes again. This time it was Jasper who leaned in.

"Ahem." Luca cleared his throat, startling Jasper and Freya, as he entered the room, "Mom told me to bring these to you." He laid some clothes on the couch.

"Thanks." Freya tried to compose herself, "Where's the bathroom?"

"Up the stairs, second door on the left." Luca pointed, not making eye contact with Jasper or Freya.

"Thank you." She nodded to Luca, then looked at Jasper, "I'll be right back." She grabbed the clothes then headed upstairs.

"I thought you were calling her here for information, not to have a make-out session on our couch." Luca snarked.

"That wasn't the intention. It just happened." Jasper defended himself, "We have this connection." He explained, "Maybe it's the whole being the same in a world that's not our own, I don't know." He looked at Luca for some kind of explanation, though he knew Luca couldn't give it.

"Looks like you both are fitting in just fine in this world that's not your own." Luca responded.

Jasper stared at him. He couldn't understand why Luca was acting this way. He imagined Luca might have made some kind of joke or comment about it. Instead, he was just being rude. He went ahead and changed the conversation to see if it would shift Luca's mood.

"She said a woman named Camille did that to her. Supposedly she is like us, but she is dark. Those of us who are like her travel to different worlds to spread their influence." Jasper explained what Freya had told him to Luca.

"Let me go get mom. She needs to hear this." Luca's tone changed some, but there was still a tinge of attitude hidden in his voice.

Zara came upstairs, but without Luca. He must have stayed down to finish things up.

"So, what's going on? Luca tried to explain." She questioned Jasper, sitting beside him on the couch.

Jasper told her what Freya had told him. As he finished, Freya entered the room. Zara patted the couch for her to come and sit by her, Luca must have also told her about the whole kissing thing. Freya sat on the other side of Zara. She was now cleaned up and seemed to be calmer than she was when she arrived.

"Jasper was telling me about Camille." Zara turned and faced Freya, "What all can you tell me about her?"

Freya looked at Jasper.

"It's okay. You can trust her." Jasper assured her.

"I really don't know all that much." She said as she sunk into the couch. "I am still learning about all of this too. I know that Camille is like us, but that she is from a faction that wants to corrupt others."

"What are we?" Jasper couldn't hold it in anymore, "I keep hearing we're not from this world, but no one gives it a name."

"Honestly," Freya shrugged, "I've not found out an exact definition of what we are. We have been called different things throughout time. Some civilizations thought of us as Gods and Goddesses, then Angels and Demons, and other creatures along that mindset. Most of those words are way off, at least from what I've gathered. The current term I'm hearing is just more generalized, we're being referred to as Celestial beings."

Jasper didn't know what to say to that. He just sat there and soaked in what he was just told. He thought by now the shock of everything would have worn off, but here he was acknowledging the thought that he was known to some as a Celestial being.

"Freya, if you're up to it," Zara paused as she watched Luca enter the room and sit down distanced from everyone, then she continued, "we had something we wanted to discuss with you."

"Okay," Freya sat up and nodded, "but I don't know how much help I can be. I've already told you everything I know." She looked at Jasper quizzingly.

"It's something I need help with." He paused, looking at Luca, wondering how much he should tell her, "When I found out the truth, I was given what my mom had left for me. She left a note that I should practice my energy work. She said that I should be able to manipulate it and extend it out of my body. That with training, I should eventually be able to do it without even thinking. Right now, the only energy work I can do involves outside forces. When I am doing the Protection Ritual, I am drawing from the ancestors and the items around me. Sure, it's my energy it manifests as, but it's not my doing. Also, it drains and exhausts me. I have no idea how to call my energy out on my own. Let alone manipulate and extend it out."

"Now that you mention it," Freya sat up, "I have heard something about that. I attempted it, but I had no luck. So, I just shrugged it off as a myth."

"Oh," Jasper slunk back, "so you don't know how I could train it."

"I didn't say that. I just said I couldn't do it." She looked at Zara, "If you have an area where we can work in, then I can try and teach him. Maybe since his mother says he can do it, he will be able to succeed where I could not."

"That's what Luca was in the basement finishing up." Zara filled her in, "Is everything good to go?" She asked Luca.

"Yep," Luca stood up, "but I'm worn out. I think I am going to go on to bed, if that's okay?" Then he headed off, not bothering to wait for a response.

"I am actually quite tired myself." Freya began to stretch.

"Oh, yes, of course." Zara stood up. "Let me go get you some stuff to make you comfortable."

"I guess I'll head upstairs then." Jasper began to get up.

"Actually," Freya spoke up, "would you mind sleeping down here with me? I really don't want to be alone tonight."

Jasper stood there, not knowing what to do. He felt like he should go talk to Luca after everything. He also felt like there was a connection with Freya and that he should stay and help her feel safe.

"I can go ahead and get you a blanket and pillow too, Jasper." Zara said as she put some on the couch for Freya, "You can make a pallet on the floor."

Jasper understood, so these were the types of subtle hints that moms dropped. "Okay, sure."

Zara brought out more pillows and covers. Jasper laid them out for him to get comfortable. It didn't help much, and it wasn't just because he hadn't gone upstairs to change out of the clothes he had been in all day. He had, yet again, been involved in a day full of information overload. Freya would potentially be able to train him, but she also informed him about a sinister force. Camille, or one of her followers, must have been who he saw cloaked and attacking the clan. He now knew people like him were currently being referred to as Celestial beings, but still didn't actually know what he was. Then, on top of it all, there was the moment shared between him and Freya.

Jasper also wondered about Luca, he felt terrible that he hadn't gone upstairs to fill him in. He also felt like after Luca became moody, maybe it was best to sleep in another room to give him space for a bit. Surely things would be better in the morning. After clearing as much of his thoughts as he could, he began to drift off.

Jasper was back standing in the field, he was beginning to get better at knowing when Luna was contacting him through his dreams. He stood and waited for her to appear, which she eventually did.

"Jasper." She greeted him eagerly.

"Luna." He nodded back. "Have you remembered more?"

"Yes," She replied, "but it's only because of what you just found out. I remember an evil force. Her name was Camille."

"Freya told me about her." Jasper interjected.

"Freya?" Luna asked.

"Yeah, she's like us. She actually found me after the vision you gave me." Jasper told her about the first time he met Freya.

"Interesting." Luna had a curious look to her face.

"She's actually with me now. She has agreed to help me with training." Jasper continued.

"Has she now?" Luna asked, her face still held its inquisitive look. It was clear she was lost in thought.

"Can I ask something?" Jasper didn't register the curiosity written all over Luna's face.

"Sure, though I cannot promise I will know the answer. At least not yet." Luna said sincerely.

"I asked Freya what we are. She said that she had found out we were once referred to, in ancient societies, as Gods, Goddesses, Angels, Demons, and so on. She said that now we are being referred to as Celestial beings, but that the actual knowledge eludes her as to what we are. So, my question for you is, what are we?" Jasper pleadingly asked Luna.

Luna grinned and slowly shook her head, "This is something I can answer, but I am not sure you will appreciate the answer."

"Please?" Jasper stepped towards her.

"Very well." She smiled, "We do not have a word that defines us."

"What?" Jasper stumbled, "How can that be?"

She laughed softly, "It is something with certain civilizations that choose to label and constrain themselves. Our way of thinking is, once you label something, you restrain it to that position. We just are." She threw her arms out, staring off in awe. "Look at what you've been taught by your clan. The only thing that is different between you and the others on this planet is that this world was never hidden from you." She looked back at Jasper softly, "Words have power, you know this. Do you really want to live a life defined by a single word? Or, do you want to live a life full of endless possibilities?" Luna smiled brightly.

"When you put it like that," Jasper looked all around, it was like he was seeing things for the first time, "I want the endless possibilities." He looked up and smiled back at Luna. "Does that mean anyone can be like us then?" Jasper asked.

"No." Luna shook her head, "We are different than most. This world is not our birth home, though our planets are similar."

"So, then, where did we come from?" Jasper, for some reason slightly worried, enquired further.

Luna must have noticed, because her face stayed calm and warm as she talked, "We come from the same creator that every other life form in this vast and unlimited universe comes from. In that, we are all connected. We just got blessed with the gifts and potentials that we possess." Her face became more serious, "But with these gifts comes a higher call to protect those who cannot protect themselves. Not everyone chooses to answer that call. Some bend to the corruption of evil and help spread its influence."

"Like Camille?" Jasper asked.

"Yes, like Camille." She replied, then composed herself back to the warm, inviting presence she normally was, "Don't worry, though. Trust yourself, follow your mother's instructions, and you will prevail above all of this. Soon we will all know more." She stopped and looked around, "For now, I must go. We will meet again." She promised.

"Wait." Jasper reached out his hand as if to call for her to stop, "One last thing."

She stopped, but Jasper could tell she was beginning to fade, "Yes?"

"Is there a way for me to access whatever this is, so I can continue training while my body is resting?" Jasper asked her. He figured if he could train while dreaming, it could speed along the process. Also, it could come in handy to be able to have some type of control over the dream realm.

"How do you think I come to you at night?" Luna laughed, "Jasper, you are the one doing this. Not me."

Then he realized why she was fading away. She was waking up.

"But how?" Jasper wondered.

"It must be a taste of your abilities. You must be able to call people to your dreams. This should be able to evolve into other traits, if you practice. Here." She threw him a stone, "This stone is said to help those like you with this ability, to learn to control it."

Jasper caught the stone. He looked up to tell her thanks, but she was gone. The stone glowed white in his hands and radiated warmth from within it. Jasper put the stone in his pocket. He began to feel a tug. He looked at his body, it was vanishing. He figured he must be waking up, but now he knew that he could work on coming back to this area. He grinned, full of euphoria, as he vanished from the field.

CHAPTER ELEVEN

Jasper woke up stretching, his body was not loving him for sleeping on the floor. As he continued stretching, he looked around. Freya was no longer on the couch. For a moment, he let himself worry that she had left, but then he heard laughter coming from the kitchen.

"Oh," Zara came from around the corner, laughing, "look who's finally awake."

"Yeah." Jasper continued stretching out, "Sleeping on the floor is not a wonderful experience."

Eventually, he got up and joined the girls in the kitchen. They all three sat down to eat and plan out their day. This would be the first day of training.

"Where's Luca?" Jasper asked.

"He went out on a walk, to recharge and prepare for training." Zara said as she sat down at the table, "I had a talk with Freya and Luca while you were asleep."

"Oh?" Jasper asked, looking at both Freya and Zara.

"You've always been a quick study when it comes to our teachings, I think you need to focus on what your mother has written for you to do. Luca and I will begin his training in an area we have set up in the woods." Zara explained.

"But what about me? I have no advanced training." Jasper understood he needed to train as his mom asked, but he also needed to be able to protect himself.

"Something tells me that if you can achieve what your mother has asked, then you will surpass anything our clan could ever teach you." Zara replied. "Sure, we can throw up shields and throw an energy blast. Some of us can even handle the elements to some degree, but that comes with severe, and sometimes life costing, consequences. Let's not kid ourselves, though. If you can manipulate your energy the way you explained, then it will surpass anything we could do."

"She's right." Freya replied.

Jasper understood what they were saying. Zara was right. If he could master what his mom explained and progress to unlocking whatever abilities he had, then he would surpass anything the clan's teachings have ever hypothesized possible. Yet, he also remembered how drained Freya got when she brought the crab back to life. Was there a consequence to his abilities too?

"What about what you did to that crab?' Jasper began, "After you did it, you were severely drained."

"Yes, you're right, but what I did was much greater than fighting. I'm almost sure our energy level is higher than those around us on this planet. As you know, we also have natural abilities, we are not all the same. Giving life cannot happen without a cost. There is no way I could bring life to a human, or anything close to that level, any time soon. If I would attempt it, I would most likely take my own life in the process." Freya explained. "I think it's the universe's way of keeping everything in balance. We may be able to do more, but we can easily suffer the same fate as those around us if we overexert ourselves too soon."

"Knowing this," Zara spoke up, "brings more importance to your training. We need you at your best. Wasting time on something you will soon be able to do without even thinking about it, is not wise."

"Okay, Zara," Jasper gave in, "if you think that is our best plan."

"I do." Zara replied.

"Then let's do it." Jasper still had some concerns, but Zara and Freya did bring up valid points. Hopefully, they were right.

After they finished eating, Zara led Freya and Jasper to the basement and made sure they had everything they would need. Then she said her goodbyes and headed off to go train with Luca.

"Okay," Jasper turned to look at Freya, "where do we begin?"

"Don't get too ahead of yourself." She laughed, "First, you have to believe you can do this. We cannot begin if you have doubt in yourself. You are used to having to burn something, crush something, or some sort of other action that involves drawing energy from things around you. Those things help, yes, but we don't require them as much as someone like Zara or Luca might. The thing is, you can do it on your own. Where they need to use those tools to be able to pull most of this off, it's just like an extra charge for us. You just need to believe in and trust yourself."

"I want to believe it, I really do." Jasper was telling the truth, he wasn't lying. "How do I do it?"

"Here," Freya took Jasper's hand and walked him to some pillows on the floor, "let's sit down. You need to meditate, set yourself free, and break the rules that bind you."

Jasper sat down across from Freya and crossed his legs. He began to grab some incense to light to help him.

"No extras, just you." Freya swatted his hand.

"Right," Jasper drew his hand back, "sorry. Now what?"

"Clear your mind." Freya instructed Jasper, "Let your mind take you away. Go to a place where anything is possible. Once you are there, do it."

"Do what?" Jasper opened one eye.

"Anything." Freya encouraged.

Jasper did as she asked. He closed his eyes, cleared his mind as best he could, and tried to envision an environment where he could see himself doing anything. After what seemed like forever, a room began taking shape. Jasper watched as the darkness faded away, and the room took form. Then he realized he knew this place, it was Luca's bedroom.

As he walked around the area, he wondered why he would have thought of Luca's bedroom as the place where anything was possible. Then he heard voices, they were faint and hard to make out. Jasper walked around the room, trying to track where they were coming from. As he walked towards the door, things began to change, and something started taking shape in front of the door. Jasper froze, it was him and Luca. Now he was confused, even more.

He stood there watching, wondering what was going on. Then he noticed what they were talking about and realized he remembered this. It was the day they snuck off to the beach. The day he made that sigil out of his energy. He continued watching, feeling a little uncomfortable staring at himself and Luca. He wondered why he felt that way. It was just him and Luca, but he felt like he was invading in some way.

Jasper watched as he opened the portal, then made the sigil, and how he and Luca freaked out about it. He still had no idea how he did it. After he and Luca walked through the portal, it closed. Once the portal closed, the room began fading away back into darkness. Jasper opened his eyes.

"So?" Freya walked over to Jasper.

"Well, something happened, but it wasn't what you wanted me to do?" Jasper answered.

"What happened?" Freya was curious.

"It's hard to explain. I still can't understand it myself."

He answered.

"No worries." She smiled and held out her hand to pull Jasper up, "We will try again tomorrow."

"Tomorrow? I'm okay to try again now." Jasper replied.

"Jasper." she stopped and looked at him, "You know you were in a trance for hours, right?"

"What?" Jasper was shocked, he couldn't understand how he was in a trance that long. It had only felt like maybe thirty minutes at most.

"Yeah, I had figured you were able to do it and were practicing." She paused for a moment, staring at Jasper as a smirk arose on her face, "This is very interesting."

"It's definitely something." Jasper wondered why Freya was smiling like she was, "Are Zara and Luca back yet?"

"I don't know." Freya's smirk went away, "I've been down here waiting for you to come out of your meditation."

"Let's go see if they're here." Jasper began walking to the stairs, "Maybe they had a better first day than we did."

Freya nodded and followed behind Jasper. When they got upstairs, they heard Zara and Luca enter through the front door. They were both laughing with each other. Hopefully, that meant they had a better day than Jasper and Freya did. Jasper walked around the corner as Zara and Luca were heading towards the kitchen.

"Hey, guys. How was training?" Jasper asked, in need of some good news.

"Good. What about you guys?" Zara asked.

"Confusing. This is going to take some time to achieve."

Jasper replied as he looked at Luca to gauge how his mood was. He wondered if Luca was back to normal today.

"Hey mom, I think I'm going to head on to bed. I'm beat after today. Love you." Luca gave Zara a hug then headed upstairs.

"Okay, sweetie, love you too. Are you sure you're not hungry?" She was too late, Luca was already gone.

"Is everything okay?" Freya asked Zara.

"Oh, that?" Zara smiled, "Yeah, it was just a long day." She walked to the kitchen, "Are you guys hungry? I can make something."

"Actually," Freya spoke up, "I'm pretty worn out. Do you mind if I go take a shower?"

"Oh sure, go right ahead." Zara looked at Jasper, "What about you? You hungry?"

Jasper turned his focus from the stairs back to Zara, "Oh, I never pass up on a good meal." He poked fun.

"Good. Me too." Zara turned and got started, "Take a seat, I'll whip something up really quick."

Jasper took a seat at the table and waited as Zara cooked something for the two of them. He wondered what was actually up with Luca, he was acting strangely. Jasper worried he had done something to make him mad. They were getting along so well. Then out of nowhere, his mood changed, and he began dodging Jasper. Zara walked over to the table, with food in hand, and took a seat.

"Zara?" Jasper asked, "Have I done something to make Luca mad?"

"Why do you ask that?" Zara questioned.

"Well, I feel as if we have grown close since I have been here. Lately, though, it seems as if he is going above and beyond to not be around me." Jasper explained, "If I did something, I never meant to. I would like to fix it."

"You boys are something else." Zara smiled, "It's been a while since I've seen Luca as happy as he was while you guys hung around one another." She looked down, her smile went away. "Luca is dealing with something right now. If what I think is true, then you guys will work it out." She smiled again, "Just give it time. Things like this have a way of sneaking up on you without you even being aware. Just knowing that you have seen the difference and want to fix it gives me the hope I need."

Jasper was confused. What was Zara talking about? Whatever she was talking about, she did acknowledge something was eating at Luca. At the same time, she was telling Jasper to be patient. He didn't like this game, but he would play if it meant getting Luca back.

"Okay, I guess that works." Jasper began thinking about his meditation today.

"Something else on your mind?" Zara noticed Jasper was lost in thought.

"Actually, yeah." Jasper began, "Today, Freya had me meditate. She explained I needed to break the beliefs I had and believe I can do what my mom said. Instead of doing that, I relived a memory. Or I visited it, I'm not sure."

"Explain." Zara said.

"I was supposed to go somewhere that I pictured anything was possible. Instead, I was taken to Luca's room. As I wandered around, I saw Luca and myself talking. It was the day we went to the beach, and I used the sigil to look through the portal. Then after we walked through the portal, I came back. I thought I was in the trance for maybe half an hour, but I was in it for hours." Jasper finished, looking at Zara for answers.

"Well, while some of what you explained is definitely interesting, and I would definitely like to know if it continues to happen, let's look at it like this too. You were told to go somewhere you felt like anything was possible. It makes sense you would subconsciously choose the place where you first did what you thought was impossible. Now being an observer on it, that's unique. I have not heard of something like that before. I think what your subconscious is trying to tell you is to get into the mindset, emotional state, headspace, whatever you were feeling at that moment again, and let loose." Zara tried to answer what she could but was also curious about Jasper's meditation experience.

Jasper took what she said and thought about it. She did make good points, but Jasper did not know what allowed him to be able to make the sigil in the first place. He would have to find out what the link was that allowed him to be able to pull something like that off.

"Thanks, Zara." Jasper went back to eating.

"Anytime." Zara did the same.

Jasper wanted to tell her about something else on his

mind, but he didn't want to plant doubt if there was no need to. Luna had visited him. She told him that he was the one calling her in his dreams, then gave him the stone to be able to practice. Yet, Freya said that they didn't need to use other items to be able to practice. He wondered why Luna would give him something, but Freya would contradict that very notion by saying it was a waste to use anything to help. Something didn't add up, but Jasper didn't want to make Zara question Freya if it was just something in Jasper's head. After all, he had no reason not to trust Freya.

Ultimately, Jasper decided to keep it to himself for now. Once they were done eating, Zara took the dishes and Jasper went upstairs to take a shower. He went into Luca's room to grab some clothes, he wanted to test the waters, but Luca was already asleep. He quietly grabbed his clothes then snuck back out.

While in the shower, Jasper had an idea. Maybe if he couldn't get Luca to speak to him in this realm, he could get Luca to talk to him in the dream realm. It would take practice, but it would be worth it to get Luca back. It was settled. Jasper would train with Freya during the day. Then at night, he would teach himself to access the dream realm and try to fix things with Luca.

Jasper finished his shower, then headed downstairs. Zara must have pulled out an air mattress for him because there was one sitting where he had slept the night before. He would have to thank her for that. His body would appreciate it. He got in bed and held the stone in his hand. Jasper waited for his body to give in to sleep and his mind to drift into the dream realm. Night one of training would soon begin.

CHAPTER TWELVE

"What am I doing wrong?" Jasper was aggravated.

Days had come and gone, but yet no progress was being made. He was following Freya's instructions to the finest detail, but nothing. He just kept going back to the same memory over and over. He knew every second of the memory by heart at this point, all except how he was able to create the sigil.

"Breathe." Freya walked over to him. "You'll get there."

"I'm not so sure about that." Jasper pulled back, "Maybe my mother was wrong about me. Maybe I'm not meant to be able to do what she thinks I can." He turned from her.

"You've been off lately." Freya looked at Jasper, "It's like you're only half here, but not fully." She stepped closer to Jasper putting her hand on his back, "What's on your mind?"

Freya was right, Jasper did have a lot on his mind. He was

still keeping his nightly practice sessions of working on controlling the dream realm a secret. He also had a part of his mind busy on trying to figure out how to fix the unknown issue between himself and Luca. On top of that, he was constantly worried about his father, while also stressing about being able to do what his mother tasked him with.

"It's just so much. Everything is weighing down on me." Jasper decided to not open up.

"Let's sit down." Freya held her hand out, "Look, Jasper, we've been working together for a while now. I'd like to think we've grown to become friends." she smiled, "As your friend, I would like to say that you suck at lying."

"This pep talk is going great." Jasper huffed.

"Who said this was going to be a pep talk?" She laughed, "Okay, fine. Look, if we have any chance of you pulling this off, then we need to be open with one another. You're not the only one being closed off."

"What do you mean?" Jasper looked at Freya.

"I like to keep things light and fun. Why do I have to tell people my whole life story? Personally, I think it insinuates certain things when you share something that private. I've never stayed anywhere long enough to let myself risk a connection like that. But, if it'll help you become more open with me, then here goes." She took a deep breath then blew it out. "I've been on my own for a long time now. I, like you, was adopted at a young age. Someone found me lost in the woods, and I was placed in a home until a family took me in. They loved and cared for me so much." Her eyes began to fill with water, "I didn't know anything about who, or what, I was. As I grew up, I started doing things that others could not. One day I came home, and my family was gone. The house was demolished. After running for a while, a clan took me in. They taught me many things, but eventually it became evident that I was something else. Their Elders searched for ways to help me. Their search ended when they found Camille. She posed as a pure and kindred spirit, but that changed once she entered the clan grounds. Camille slaughtered each and every one of them. I had no choice but to run, and I've been running ever since.

"Freya," Jasper reached out to her, "I had no idea."

"You wouldn't." She sat up, shaking her head and smiling, "I have no reason to tell people. I have lived my life fearing to let people in. I never stay in the same place long. I refuse to let anyone else die because of me."

"I get it." Jasper looked down, he knew he needed to open up. "I was given a vision of Lyteshaed being attacked by a hooded figure. I saw everyone from my clan dead. Some were no longer bodies, but just piles of ashes. I saw my dad being attacked, and froze as I watched an attack from this shrouded entity be launched directly at me." He looked up at Freya, "I have to keep them safe. I can't let them die because of me. I have to follow my mom's instructions. If I can't do this, then I am stuck. Every day wasted is another day risking the clan's safety."

Jasper watched Freya as she took in the information that

he just gave her. It was as if something registered in her, and at that moment, she changed. She stood up and walked to the other side of the room. Jasper couldn't tell what was going on. Then Freya walked back over to Jasper.

"I think we are done for the day, but tomorrow." She stopped and smiled, "Tomorrow is the day. I have an idea. It goes against what I've been saying, but it might just work." Then she turned and walked off, heading upstairs.

Jasper stood in the basement, watching Freya exit through the door. Whatever she realized, it changed her. The way she talked to Jasper filled him with hope. He believed her. For some reason, he too now thought tomorrow would be his lucky day. He let out a sigh of relief, a weight leaving his chest, then walked upstairs.

"How was today?" Zara was preparing food for everyone.

"I think we had a breakthrough." Freya told her, "Something tells me tomorrow is the day." She winked at Jasper.

"How was your day?" Jasper asked.

"Oh, it was good. Luca is really doing well with learning these new techniques." Zara smiled as Luca walked in and sat at the table.

"She's being boastful. I'm doing okay." Luca smiled as he sat down.

Zara had been correct about being patient. Luca had been coming back around and joining the group. It wasn't what it used to be, but it was progress. Jasper could take that.

"It's what parents do, they brag." Jasper teased as he joined Freya and Luca at the table.

Zara finished up and joined them too. They all ate and talked about their day. Jasper did more listening than he did talking in the conversation. With him and Luca doing better, he had been wanting to show him about the dream realm. With things looking up with Freya, he wanted to keep the momentum going. He had a pretty good hold of entering and exiting the realm but had no idea on how to invite or bring people. Somehow he was able to bring Luna over, but, just like with the sigil, he had no idea how he was doing it. He had a plan, though. If Luca would take the stone to bed with him, then he may be able to bring him over that way.

Jasper planned while everyone ate, waiting for the perfect time to be able to give Luca the stone. He had to do it without letting Zara or Freya know. He still wanted this ability to be kept a secret. Soon everyone was finished. Freya got up to help Zara. This was Jasper's moment.

"I think I'm going to go get ready for bed." Luca said after rinsing his dish.

"Oh, I'll go ahead and follow you up and get my stuff too. I don't want to wait too late and wake you up when I decide to change." Jasper laughed.

Luca nodded, gave his mom a hug, and began heading upstairs. Jasper washed his dish and followed after him.

"Hey." Jasper said as he walked into Luca's room.

"Hey." Luca standoffishly replied.

"Look, I know something is going on between us right now, but I want to show you something." Jasper reached in his pocket and pulled out the stone Luna had given him.

"A stone?" Luca looked at the stone and then Jasper with a puzzled expression.

"Yeah, a stone, but it's more than that. There's something I want to show you." Jasper hinted.

"What's that?" Luca was still being standoffish.

"Well, I can't say. I need to show you." He held out the stone for Luca to take it. "I need you to trust me."

Luca stared at Jasper, but he didn't reach out for the stone. Jasper looked at him and sighed.

"Look, I want to fix things. I want to share things with you again." He placed the stone on Luca's bedside table, "If you want the same, then when you lay down take this stone to bed with you. If you're done, then don't. I'll know either way." Jasper grabbed some clothes, "I just hope I know which one you will choose." Then he walked out of Luca's room, heading towards the bathroom to change.

When Jasper walked out of the bathroom and headed towards the living room, he saw that Luca's bedroom door was closed. There was no way he could know if Luca had taken the stone or not, but he hoped for the best. Jasper headed on downstairs.

The lights were all off, except for a lamp here and there to give some light. Jasper figured Zara must have gone on to bed. Freya was lying on the couch, almost asleep when

Jasper climbed onto the air mattress.

"There he is." She said with a smile, her eyes closed.

"Sorry, I was talking with Luca." Jasper replied, climbing under the covers.

"That's good." Freya rolled over. "Get your sleep, tomorrow's a big day."

Jasper wondered what her idea was. She seemed to be so sure that he would be able to perform the task tomorrow without question. Although it ate at him, he let his mind empty itself. Tonight was going to be all about trying to fix things between him and Luca. Jasper let his mind drift off into a deep sleep.

Jasper stood in the field for what seemed like an eternity. The longer time ticked on, he became more aware of the potential reality that Luca had no intention of working things out. Then, as he was about to give up, he saw a wrinkle off in the distance. He walked closer. As he approached it, the wrinkle began to open up. A tear began to form in the fabric of the dream realm. Out stepped a shocked and confused Luca. Jasper perked up with a grin.

"You came." Jasper now knew there was a chance to fix things.

"Of course I did" Luca looked around, "What is this place?"

"It's the field where I perform the annual Ritual of Protection." Jasper explained.

"So, we are awake?" Luca asked, still trying to figure it out.

"No." Jasper shook his head, "This is the dream realm."

"What?" Luca was shocked.

"Apparently, it's an ability of mine. I can control the dream realm. I can also invite people to become aware of themselves while in the dream realm." Jasper was proud of his ability.

"So, you could spy on people while they're dreaming?" Luca suspiciously looked at Jasper, "You've not spied on my dreams, have you?"

"No, I can't spy on people's dreams. Though, I bet if I work on this more, I may be able to eventually." Jasper looked at Luca, "Why? Are you hiding something?" he playfully asked.

"No." Luca blushed, "Just making sure I don't have a pervy dream stalker to worry about." He teased.

"Jasper the Pervy Dream Stalker." Jasper waved his hand across the air as he spoke, "I like it."

They both broke out in laughter. Jasper missed this, both of them getting along and making jokes. It was like old times.

"Luca?" Jasper's laughter quieted down, "What did I do to make you mad? I swear I didn't mean to do anything to hurt or upset you."

"It's nothing you did." Luca looked down at the ground.

"Then what?" Jasper stepped towards him.

"Just something I have to deal with on my own." Luca looked up, "But we're good."

"I'm glad to hear that, but please know I'm here for

you if you need to talk.' Jasper replied.

"Thanks." Luca smiled, "Now enough of that. We're in the dream realm." He looked around, "What is there to do in here?"

"I've honestly not tried anything yet. I've been busy working on being able to freely enter. I didn't know if the stone idea would even work to allow you in." Jasper paused, "By the way, if you want to be able to come here, then you need to keep the stone a little longer until I can control that part better."

"Sounds good." Luca patted his pocket.

"I have an idea of what we can do." Jasper smiled mischievously, "Why don't you show me what you've been learning?" Jasper took his hand, palm facing down, and waved it out in front of him making a circle. As he did, a circle appeared surrounding them both, "I didn't know if that would even work." He laughed, "First to knock the other out of the circle wins?"

"Sure, but can you handle the defeat?" Luca smirked.

"I should ask you the same?" Jasper teased back.

"We can't hurt each other in here, can we?" Luca took a serious note for a moment.

"There's only one way to find out." Jasper shrugged.

"Let's do this without powers then. I don't need to go hurting you before you ever get to see what you're capable of." Luca joked.

Jasper agreed. He was up for finding out what all transferred into the real world from the dream realm but also didn't want to hurt one another. They both took their stance and began. As they sparred, it was like they were closing the gap between them.

Luca charged at Jasper, Jasper took a side step, and Luca went flying to the ground. He was right at the edge of the circle.

"Almost." Jasper laughed as he held out a hand to help Luca up.

Luca reached up to grab Jasper's hand. Once he had ahold, he pulled Jasper down to the ground. As Luca pulled him down, he rolled, causing Jasper to cross the circle and land on his back with Luca laughing on top of him.

"What was that?" Luca laughed, "I'm sorry, I couldn't hear you over the sound of your defeat."

"Fair enough." Jasper laughed back, "You got me."

Their laughter began to die down and was replaced by silence. Jasper looked up at Luca and Luca down at him. They're eyes locked. Jasper's heartbeat began to quicken. He could feel Luca's breath brushing against his face. Jasper felt Luca's arm brush his as Luca balanced himself, causing goosebumps to travel through Jasper's body. Jasper scanned what he could of Luca's body. When Jasper relocked eyes with Luca, he was looking down at him with a soft smile on his face. Jasper smiled back. Luca chuckled and then lowered his body, barely touching Jasper's, and pushed himself off the ground. As Luca dusted himself off, Jasper lay there wondering what had just happened.

"So how goes everything with you and Freya?" He held

out his hand to help Jasper up.

"What do you mean?" Jasper asked as he stood up.

"I see the way you two look at one another." Luca teased.

"I don't know." Jasper blushed, "Sure, I have wondered if there's a mutual attraction. You know, if we could be more than friends." He looked at Luca, "But it's not that simple." He looked back down as he swiped at the dirt on his pants.

"Sure it is." Luca playfully jabbed Jasper's arm, "You just got to take a chance sometimes." He looked at Jasper rubbing his arm, "Oh come on, I didn't hit you that hard."

"I think it's from the other hits you landed." Jasper laughed, rolling his sleeve up to reveal a mark, "Yep, that's going to bruise."

"Well, look at this way. At least you'll be able to know if it carries over to the real world." Luca paused, "Wow, that's weird. Real world." He looked at Jasper, "This is going to take a while to get used to."

"I get it." Jasper laughed, "Just don't mention it to any-one. I want to keep it a secret."

"I got you." Luca assured.

"Thanks," Jasper was both relieved and excited, "I'm glad to have you back." He threw his hand over Luca's shoulder.

"Whoa!" Luca held out his hands in panic, "What's hap-pening?" he watched as his hands began to fade away.

"Don't worry." Jasper laughed, "It just means we are waking up." He showed Luca how he was fading too.

"Catch you on the flip side." Jasper smiled brightly as they both faded away, leaving behind nothing but an empty field.

CHAPTER THIRTEEN

Jasper sat up on the mattress. He was on cloud nine. He had fixed things with Luca, and Freya was optimistic about today's training. What was there to not be happy about? Jasper got up and walked into the kitchen to eat with everyone before they all went their separate ways. When Jasper sat down, he rolled up his sleeve to see if his arm was bruised.

"What happened to your arm?" Zara walked over and checked out his arm.

"I don't know it must have happened in my sleep." Jasper faked a sense of shock while trying not to smile.

Out of the corner of his eye, Jasper saw Luca slip a smirk. He quickly wiped it away so no one would catch it.

"What about my bruises?" Luca pouted, "Aren't you going to check me?" he teased.

"Oh, hush." Zara waved her hand in the air, "I get it,

overprotective." She sat down at the table.

"I thought it was adorable." Freya warmly smiled.

"Thank you, Freya." Zara nodded.

"You're welcome. Could you check this spot on my side?" She laughed.

"Oh, everyone's a comedian." Zara huffed.

They all busted out laughing. It had been a while since they all sat at the table and joked and laughed like this. It was nice. They all finished eating. Luca and Zara left to go their way, while Freya and Jasper headed to the basement to begin their training.

"So, what is this big idea you have? What is going to suddenly enable me to do what I have not been able to the entire time we've been training?" Jasper asked teasingly.

"You'll see." Freya smiled.

Jasper watched as Freya searched through Zara's supplies she had stored in the basement. He wondered what she was doing. She dug through different areas. She knew what she was searching for. Once she had everything, Freya walked over to Jasper, with her arms full, and sat down in front of him.

"Sit." She nodded to the pillow in front of her.

"You said we didn't need supplies to do this?" Jasper asked, confused as he sat down.

"You're right, I did." She set everything down in front of them, "Then I realized something." She looked up at him with a smile, but there was an emotion hidden in the smile that Jasper couldn't make out.

"What's that?" He asked, looking at everything she had grabbed.

"You were trained for many years to use this stuff." She gestured. "To all of a sudden be told you don't need it, was maybe a bit of a stretch. So today, we're using these to help you. As you progress, we will remove an item." She explained.

"I guess that makes sense. So how long do you think it will take?" Jasper asked, inspecting the items further.

"Oh," Freya slapped Jasper's hand as he reached for one of the stones, "you're going to have this down by tonight."

"What? Tonight?" Jasper was shocked.

"Yes, tonight." Freya mimicked, "Think of these items as a type of jump start. I tried to get you to start without a charge. Once you get going, your innate ability to do this should take over."

"But, you can't even do this." Jasper looked at her, puzzled, "How are you expecting me to?"

"Well, Jasper," she stared at him, blankly, "I didn't have a super-secret journal left by my mother, which gave me special instructions to follow."

"Okay, you got me there." Jasper laughed.

Freya shook her head, then she got serious and focused on setting everything up. Jasper watched her, there was a green candle, fluorite, lapis lazuli, and thyme. Once she was done, she looked back up at Jasper.

"Ready?" She asked.

"Ready." He nodded his head.

"Here goes. Close your eyes." She lit a match, "Fire to focus, green to accomplish." She lit the candle, "Fluorite to boost, lapis lazuli to stimulate." She placed the stones on each side of the candle, "And thyme to awaken the mind." She sprinkled thyme over the candle and stone.

A puff of smoke rose into the air, and the flame grew brighter. Jasper, with his eyes still closed, inhaled deeply as the smoke flowed into him. At first, nothing happened, and Jasper felt defeated. Then as he began to open his eyes, he felt it. Something had awakened inside of him. Freya saw it too.

"It's okay, you can open them now." She said.

"What was that?" He asked, examining his body.

"I told you." She spoke calmly, "All you needed was a jump start."

"So, you mean I can do it now?" He held his hand up.

"You tell me. Try to bring out your energy." She replied.

Jasper concentrated on his hands. He already knew how to draw his energy out that way. The clan had taught that to everyone. It was how they activated sigils, enchanted objects, charged stones, and more. He watched as his energy streamed out of his palms and wrapped around both hands.

"Okay, now take it up your arms." Freya instructed.

Jasper concentrated. He had never had his energy go past his hands. It had never been possible to pull out that much energy. He focused his mind on the thought of it winding past his hands and around his arms. At first, it was a slow movement, but it began moving faster as it inched up his sleeve. Jasper jumped. He had done it. In his excitement, he lost focus, and the energy jolted right back into him.

"Wow, that's going to be a new feeling to get used to." He clinched and opened his hands.

"Yeah," Freya laughed, "I would assume a slower retrieval would be more beneficial."

"I just got excited." Jasper shook his hands.

"It's okay. This time though," she reached and took the lapis lazuli away, "try it without this." She encouraged Jasper.

"Okay?" Jasper was nervous but attempted it still.

Again, he quickly brought the energy to his hands. He focused as he willed it to cover his arms too.

"Great." Freya was proud of Jasper. "Now, cover your entire body."

By this point, Jasper had become confident in his ability, but he wondered how much energy he had. He questioned if he had enough to cover his body and not drain himself. Slowly, he willed the energy to cover him entirely. The thick blue energy rose past his arms, over his head, down his chest, legs, and wrapped under his feet. It was like he had a blanket over him, made entirely out of his own energy. He was surprised he could see through it clearly. He had assumed everything would get a wavy blue tint to it.

"Jasper, you're doing it!" Freya shrieked with excitement. "Now keep it going, but," she removed the fluorite.

"without this to help."

Jasper's energy thinned, it wasn't as thick as it had previously been. He now knew he could hold out this amount of energy without assistance, but he would have to train more to increase it.

"Very good." Freya praised him, "I want you to bring it to your hands, but I don't want you to absorb any in. I want you to compact it on your hands."

"What do you mean?" Jasper asked, trying to keep focusing on his energy.

"Condense it in your hands, shape it, and form it into something." Freya explained, encouraging Jasper.

Jasper nodded, he understood what she was asking. He had a handle on being able to bring it out. Without help, though, it was really thin. This would allow him to thicken it and shape it how he liked without outside help. Jasper concentrated on drawing the energy back to his hands without allowing it to enter back into him.

Slowly the energy receded back to his hands. Jasper watched as the thin flowing energy on his hand solidified, the flow of it slowing down. The thicker it grew, the heavier his hands became. Jasper focused on shaping it into the most basic thing he could think of, a ball. He brought his weighted hands together and concentrated. Freya watched in anticipation as he did. Slowly the energy swirled together. Jasper rolled his hands around, pushing and compacting. He continued until there, in his hands, sat a medium-sized ball made entirely out of his energy. It was held together by a hardened, transparent layer with his energy swirling inside. Jasper looked at Freya who was smiling as she leaned down and blew out the candle.

"Now what?" Jasper asked, looking at the ball in his hand.

"Here," Freya held her hands out, "throw it to me."

Jasper looked down, he wondered if he was going to be able to detach it from his body. There was only one way to find out. He closed his eyes, trusted his instinct, and tossed the ball. Jasper opened his eyes to watch the ball glide through the air and land right in Freya's lap.

"You did it!" she cheered, holding up the ball. "You no longer have to focus on it. It will not go anywhere."

"Really?" Jasper quit focusing on the ball, "How is this possible?"

"I'm surprised you were able to excel so quickly. This is a technique I read about but didn't think it was possible. It is said that those strong enough can conjure up and store their energy, kind of like a reservoir. You could also fill it with an attack. For example, if elements were your thing, then you could create mini elemental balls for your allies. The possibilities are really endless."

"Wow." Jasper sat there flabbergasted, not knowing what else to say.

"Here." She threw the ball back at Jasper.

"What should I do with it?" He asked.

"You can either break the layer holding it and reabsorb the energy. Or you can shrink it and store it as a mini energy booster." Freya explained.

Jasper went with shrinking it. He pushed it in the middle of his hands and rolled it, causing it to sink into itself growing smaller and smaller. Eventually, it was the size of a marble. Jasper held it up.

"I definitely have to show Luca and Zara this." He smiled, placing the energy marble in his pocket. "What else can I do?" He asked, scooting closer to Freya.

"Well, the more you practice, you should be able to do what I just said. You should also be able to, like your mother wants, shape, extend, and manipulate it all with or without breaking your tether off." She explained.

"Break my tether?" Jasper asked.

"When you threw the ball, and I said you no longer had to focus on it." She began, Jasper nodding as she continued, "You had broken your tether. The ball was no longer an extension of you. It was then its own entity. You can do other things, but not break your tether. With that, though, comes having to have greater focus because then the energy is not its own entity. It is instead an extension of you. At first, you should only be able to extend it out slightly. As you practice, and the stronger you get, the further you should be able to send it while still attached to you."

"So, what are the advantages of having the energy stay tethered to me?" Jasper asked.

"Well, for one, you're not losing energy. You only made one ball. Imagine making a group of those for your allies during a battle, it would drain you. Other advantages could be that you could make stronger shields than a sigil ever would. You could also use it to feel out rooms or areas ahead of you. Or to even carry yourself."

"You mean like levitation?" Jasper was pumped.

"Yeah, but that takes a lot of practice." Freya warned.

Jasper practiced the rest of the evening, calling out his energy and trying to extend and shape it. He would create the balls, bust them open, absorb the energy, and restart. He couldn't understand how for the past few days he had been stumped, then today he was able to pull it off without much work at all. Whatever the cause, Jasper was happy things were finally progressing. He was in the middle of creating another orb when they heard Luca and Zara arrive.

"I have an idea." Jasper mischievously grinned, holding the energy orb in his hand, "I need you to walk in front of me. Don't let on that today went as good as it did. I want to surprise them."

Freya nodded with an equal smile agreeing to help him. She helped Jasper get up so he could keep focusing on the orb in his hand. Once Jasper had his bearings, he followed behind her up the stairs.

"Any luck?" Zara asked as Freya and Jasper entered the kitchen.

"We really tried, but," she looked down and then back at Jasper, "I don't know what else I could try with him."

Jasper walked past Freya with his hands behind his back, trying hard not to lose focus or break the act they were putting on.

"Oh, Jasper, I'm sorry." Zara took a step towards them.

"Sorry for what?" Jasper smirked as he brought his hands out from behind his back.

"Wait." Luca gasped, taking a step forward, "Is that?"

"Yep." Jasper nodded, "Catch." He threw the orb in the air at them.

As it was about to land, it shattered above them, raining down pieces of Jasper's energy over both Zara and Luca. As it dropped to the floor, it became smoky and flowed directly back to Jasper. Freya looked at him with a smile. Luca and Zara both stood there with shocked faces, not knowing how to interpret what just happened.

"So," Zara finally spoke, "this means you've done it. You've completed the task set by your mom?"

"Almost, there's more. That was only part of it." Jasper looked at Luca, then back at Zara, "I have to speak with Axton."

"Well," Zara paused, "I'll have to contact the Elders and let them know. You're not to go back to Lyteshaed until this is all settled. Seeing the circumstances, though, I cannot see how they can deny a short visit." Zara began planning in her mind.

"Actually," Jasper held up his left hand, revealing the bracelet on his wrist, "I have a way to contact him without having to risk the safety of the clan."

Luca stood behind his mom smiling, he was proud of Jasper. Jasper caught his smile and nodded in appreciation. Then he explained how Axton had given him a piece of the castle and told him he could use it to bring Axton to him, but only for a short period of time. Hopefully, it would be enough time to figure out how to do what he needed to.

"You mean you want to call him now?" Zara asked, realizing at that moment how dirty she was from training.

"If there are no objections," Jasper scanned the room, "then I think the sooner we do this, the better it will be for the clan."

"Do you think he is ready?" Zara asked Freya.

"I don't know what exactly he has to do," she looked at Jasper then back at Zara, "but I've taught him all I can. So, yes, I would agree. No time like the present."

"Well," Zara looked at her clothes and then at Luca's, "you and I better go clean up. Then we can go ahead and do this." She turned and walked out of the room.

Luca nodded and walked out shortly after her. Jasper, both anxious and excited, turned and looked at Freya. Things were progressing quickly after such a long stretch of nothing. Jasper put his hands in his pocket, feeling the marble he had created. He had forgotten all about it.

"I'm going to run upstairs real quick." He told Freya, "I'll be right back."

Jasper walked out of the room, leaving Freya in the kitchen to wait for everyone to prepare for Axton's arrival. Jasper headed upstairs, he knocked on Luca's door.

"Come in." Luca called through the door.

"Sorry to bother you." Jasper walked in.

"No, you're good." Luca slipped on a clean shirt and

turned to face Jasper, "What's up?"

"I wanted to give you something." Jasper reached into his pocket and pulled out the marble.

"What is that?" Luca approached Jasper, examining the strange marble shape in his hand.

"It's a smaller, yet fuller, version of the ball I showed you and Zara earlier." He explained.

Jasper took Luca's hand, pausing as he noticed a spark of some sort when they touched. He placed it in Luca's hand.

"Think of this as an emergency energy battery." Jasper slid his hand over Luca's fingers to have them cover the marble.

"Why are you giving it to me?" Luca looked at Jasper, puzzled.

"I wanted to give it to someone I trusted. Someone who would always be by my side." Jasper smiled, "If I ever am low on energy, you'll have an extra boost to give me in a tight pinch."

"I'll keep it on me always." Luca closed his hand around the marble, slipping it into his pocket.

"Think of it this way." Jasper teased, "Now, you're stuck with me always."

"Who said that would be an issue?" Luca smirked back.

They both laughed, then finished getting ready. Once the boys were done, they headed downstairs to meet the girls.

"Ready?" Zara asked, meeting them at the base of the

steps.

"As ready as I'm going to be." Jasper replied.

Zara gestured for Jasper to head into the living room. Jasper scanned the room as they all stood in a circle. He placed the bracelet on the floor in the middle of them. His heart began to pound. He was starting to realize he was one step closer to finding his parents.

"If we all do this part, then he may be able to stay longer. Which could give me more time to figure out the next step." Jasper explained.

"What do we need to do?" Luca asked.

"We need to all channel some energy into this bracelet, then I will call for him. After that, it shouldn't be long, and he will be here." Jasper answered.

They all nodded and agreed. Then, one by one, they all bent down, and each took turns channeling a little of their own energy into the bracelet. Jasper went last. As he finished channeling his energy, he whispered Axton's name.

"Now what?" Luca asked.

"Now," Jasper replied, "we wait."

CHAPTER FOURTEEN

Everyone stood in the middle of the living room, staring at the bracelet, waiting for something to happen. Jasper began to wonder if he had forgotten a step or misunderstood the correct way to contact Axton with it. As he was about to give up hope, the bracelet began to glow.

"It's doing something." Luca pointed at it.

Everyone moved close to Jasper. Zara stood to his left, Freya to his right, and Luca behind him. They all huddled together, watching as the bracelet grew brighter. Then a dense cloud of smoke began to swirl out of it. The bracelet started to reshape itself, becoming flat and expanding. There was a bright flash of light, causing everyone to shield their eyes.

"Good evening, everyone." A voice spoke to them.

Jasper and the others had to focus their eyes after the flash. As his eyes refocused, Jasper saw Axton was now standing in the middle of the circle. Where the bracelet had been, there now laid a small platform just big enough for Axton to stand on.

"Axton," Zara composed herself, "it's great to see you."

"Same to you, Zara." Axton bowed his head, "You too, boys." He nodded to Jasper and Luca, then spotted Freya. "My apologies, but I do not believe we have met." Axton stretched out his hand to greet Freya.

"Hello there." Freya smiled politely, shaking Axton's hand, "I'm Freya," She introduced herself, "I've been helping Jasper with some of his training."

"Oh, is that so?" Axton looked at Jasper, puzzled.

"It's a long story." Jasper chuckled.

"I see." Axton cautiously scanned Freya, then turned back to Jasper with a questioning look, "What can I help you with this evening?"

"Oh," Jasper sighed, "Where to begin?"

Jasper continued to explain to Axton the events that had unfolded since he had arrived at Zara's. He told Axton about the sigil, more being revealed in the journal, and the many training sessions he has undergone. Jasper kept out information that he was only sharing with Luca, such as his ability to control the dream realm and so on. Axton just stood there, taking in all the information he was being given.

"Alright, let me see if I understand this." Axton stated, "Your mother confided in me instructions on how to find a missing piece to a necklace she left you. She then had you train to be able to unlock whatever memory wipe she did on me but did not leave instructions on how to do it?"

"That's the simplified version, yes." Jasper nodded, knowing how it all sounded.

"So," Axton turned to Freya, "do you have any idea how what he has learned is going to unlock this supposed memory block put upon me?"

"I'm sorry," Freya put her head down, "but no." She looked at everyone, "I can honestly say that I have no idea how what I have taught him and what his mom has told him even relate with one another." She looked at Jasper, "Though, I have come to be impressed by the actions he is capable of. So, if his mom says he can do it, then I believe he is able to." She smiled, placing her hand on his arm.

"Thanks, Freya." Jasper felt comfort in her belief. While he wasn't sure of himself, it was nice to know someone was.

"Well, this should be interesting then." Axton said.

"You're telling me." Jasper sighed.

"Well," Axton composed himself, "let's begin."

Jasper began charging his energy and calling it out to his hands like in his training. Luca, Zara, and Axton all watched in anticipation to see what he could do. Zara and Luca had seen an energy orb he had made, but that was it. They all stood watching in anticipation as Jasper willed the energy to flow and cover his body. He opened his eyes and began walking towards Axton, half focusing on keeping the energy out and half focusing on making Axton remember. Oddly, the closer Jasper got to Axton, the more his energy began to fade. As Jasper reached his hand out to touch Axton, about six inches before making contact, his energy completely retreated and shot back inside of him.

"What was that?" Axton asked.

"Jasper, are you okay?" Zara was concerned.

"I don't understand." Jasper regathered his footing and looked at Freya.

"Don't look at me. I'm as shocked as you." She replied.

"It's like there's some kind of barrier around him that is blocking anyone from using their energy on him." Luca suggested, staring intensely at Axton, trying to think of a way to break the barrier.

"You okay?" Freya grabbed Jasper's arm.

"Yeah, I'm good." He touched her hand, trying to hide his worry.

"Try again." She encouraged, "Maybe it was a part of the process?"

Jasper nodded and tried again. This time, instead of bringing his energy over his whole body, he concentrated on building a bigger storage on just his hands. Again, he focused on the energy and on making Axton remember. Once he was ready, he began walking towards Axton. Same as last time, though, the closer he got, the more his energy retreated. Until eventually, it shot back into him around the same distance away from Axton.

"What the hell?" Jasper was getting aggravated, both from it not working and the pain caused by his energy shooting back into him. It was as if that was also a part of the barrier. Not only did it not allow another person's energy to cross it, but it also shot it back with force to try and discourage them from trying again.

"What if you try doing the little trick you showed Luca and me?" Zara looked at Jasper, "You know the energy ball, or orb, or whatever it was. Maybe it will be enough to break through?" She recommended.

"It's worth a shot." Jasper shrugged, "Everyone might want to step back, though. If it bounces back, then it could hurt."

Zara and Freya backed away as warned, but Luca stood his ground. Jasper looked back at him, but all Luca did was smile and nod. A part of Jasper wanted to tell Luca he should back away with Zara and Freya, but a more significant part of him was happy to have Luca standing behind him. He turned and looked at Axton.

"Ready?" Jasper asked.

Axton nodded as Jasper began, for the third time, to call out his energy. He concentrated on shaping the energy in his hands. He continued compacting more and more energy into the ball. When he felt he was done, he examined what was in his hands. It was about the size of a baseball, but inside, his energy spun faster than the other balls he had made before. He focused on trying to fill the ball with the intention of making Axton remember. He brought it up to his mouth, closed his eyes, and whispered a single word.

"Memento."

Then Jasper took a breath and threw the ball directly at Axton. It was like time moved slowly as everyone stood there in Zara's living room, watching the energy ball fly from Jasper's hand towards Axton. It got closer and closer, Jasper thought it was going to make it. Then it reached the same point he had with his hand and ricocheted straight back at Jasper. It hit him with a force so strong it sent him flying into Luca and knocked them both down.

"Luca! Jasper!" Zara rushed to them.

"Jasper," Luca caught his breath, "what did I tell you about buying me dinner first?" He laughed.

"Sorry," Jasper laughed and coughed, catching his breath too, "I was caught in the moment."

"Boys, are you okay?" Zara questioned as she bent down to check on them both.

"Yeah, mom. We're fine." Luca said as Jasper rolled off the top of him, and they both stood up.

"I don't know how much more of this we should attempt. It's getting more dangerous." Zara said as she stood there, still checking out the boys.

"I agree." Axton said, "I should also note that I do not have much longer. I will have to return to the castle soon. The energy in the bracelet is beginning to fade."

"No." Jasper said, shaking himself off, "We must figure this out. I have to, it's what my mom wanted."

"Jasper," Freya walked up to him, sincerely, "maybe you're just not ready. You can try again after more training."

"No, you're wrong." Jasper shrugged Freya off of him,

his eyes beginning to fill up with water as panic rose in his chest, "The clan does not have time to wait for me to train. The longer we waste time trying to figure out these cryptic messages, the longer we are risking everyone's safety."

"Jasper…" Zara began to comfort him but was interrupted.

"Mom," Luca touched her shoulder, "let me." He walked over to Jasper, nodding for Freya to go stand by Zara. "Jasper, look at me." He put both hands on Jasper's shoulders as Jasper rose his head to look at Luca. "If you want to do this, you need to calm down." Luca explained, "Close your eyes. Remember the day we went to the beach? You did that, you did what no one else has ever dreamt possible. You can do this." He consoled Jasper, "Just calm yourself, trust your instincts, and break the barrier. Make him remember."

"You're right." Jasper nodded, wiping the back of his hand across his eyes to not let any tears fall. "Thank you." He said softly.

Luca nodded and stepped back, joining both Zara and Freya. A newly determined Jasper looked back at them, and then he turned and faced Axton.

"One last time?" Jasper asked him.

"You've got this." Axton optimistically looked back at Jasper.

Jasper grounded himself for one last attempt. He closed his eyes and quieted his mind. Jasper stood there silent, as the others watched him. He began focusing on a singular thought, he had to create something that would not only break past the barrier but would also break the block his mother had put on Axton's memory.

"He's doing something." Zara whispered.

"What is he doing?" Freya whispered, looking at Luca.

"Just watch." Luca spoke, not breaking his gaze on Jasper.

Jasper took a breath, then his hands began waving and winding through the air. To everyone watching him, it was like watching an artist paint a picture. His energy pouring out of him and floating in mid-air as he continued working. When he was finished, he opened his eyes. Jasper turned and stared at the others with a proud smile.

"I've never heard of anyone being able to do something like this." Freya spoke up.

"That sigil, I've never seen it before. What does it mean?" Zara said, examining the it.

"Go on." Luca said, his smile matching Jasper's, "Show them."

Jasper nodded and turned back to face Axton, who was just as shocked as the others at what he was looking at. Jasper gave the sigil a light push with his hand. Everyone watched as the sigil wisped through the air, heading straight for Axton. They all held their breath as the sigil reached the point where nothing else had been able to pass.

The sigil began to glow as it touched the barrier causing the barrier to shatter outwards in a burst of energy. Everyone steadied themselves as the barrier pieces flew past them, vanishing from sight. They turned to witness the sigil soaking into Axton's body. Once it was fully absorbed, Axton dropped to the ground.

"Axton!" Jasper shouted as everyone rushed to his side.

"I'm okay," Axton began to stand back up, "it's fine."

"Are you sure everything is okay?" Zara said, assisting him up.

"Yes, no need to worry." Axton patted Zara's hand on his arm, "I promise, I'm fine."

"So?" Luca asked, "Did it work?"

"It did." Axton nodded.

"But?" Jasper had caught the face Axton made.

"I'm not going to be able to tell you what you really want to know." Axton looked at Jasper, "I still have no idea who your parents are. I only know the message I am to pass on to you."

"Oh." Jasper looked down, "Well, it was worth a try. I guess I should have known it wouldn't be that easy."

"Are you okay?" Luca placed his hand on Jasper's back.

"Yeah," Jasper forced a fake smile, "I'm good." He looked at Axton, "So, what is this message you have to pass on? I'm sure your time is running low, so we should hurry and get to it."

"Okay." Axton nodded with a sigh, then began. "Your mother entrusted me with the instructions, and the location, of a missing piece for the necklace she left for you. She hid it away in a cave, about two days south of Lyteshaed."

"Great." Zara interrupted Axton, "You can give us the location, and we can teleport a small squad to retrieve it."

"It's not that easy." Axton shook his head, "She placed markers and shielded the location. She wanted to ensure no one could get the information and magically travel there. She also took steps to make sure that a lost wanderer didn't find it by accident. She made it so that if they would get close, they would unknowingly be transported to the other side of the shielding. To them, it would be like taking a simple step. Realistically they were traveling days worth of miles in that one step."

"So how do we get the item then?" Zara asked.

"It has to be Jasper that retrieves it," Axton said, turning to face Jasper, "and he has to have the necklace with him."

"Why the necklace?" Jasper asked.

"The markers." Axton explained, "The necklace will glow as you get closer to one so that you know you are on the right path. As long as you have the necklace with you, then you will be able to travel to the cave's location. You will just have to do it the old-fashioned way, and walk."

"Okay." Zara spoke up, thinking out loud, "I can get an immediate audience with the Elders, and we can assign a squadron to accompany Jasper to retrieve the item."

"No." Jasper interjected.

"No?" Zara asked, "Why?"

"The clan needs all the protection we have to offer. We cannot afford to send off a squad, when we know there is a chance of a deadly attack. I won't allow it. I can go by myself."

"Jasper." Zara replied softly, "You cannot make this journey by yourself."

"He won't be alone." Freya grabbed onto Jasper's arm, sliding close to his body, "He'll have me with him." She said, placing her head on his shoulder and smiling up at him.

"And me." Luca placed his hand on Jasper's other shoulder.

"I cannot let you guys go on this journey alone." Zara scoffed, looking at Axton who was smiling at Freya, Jasper, and Luca. "Axton?"

"Don't look at me. I'm just the messenger." Axton chuckled.

"Zara." Jasper looked at her, "We can do this." He defended his choice while trying to make her feel comfortable with the idea.

"Luca?" Zara worrisomely looked at her son.

"Mom, we will be fine." He lightly smiled. "It's his mom sending him there. Would you knowingly send me to a dangerous location?"

"No." Zara looked down, seeing where Luca was going.

"We have to go with him." Luca looked at both Freya then Jasper. "You're right. He can't go alone, but he won't allow the clan to lose protection. This is the best option."

Zara looked one last time at Axton, hoping he would say something, but there he stood smiling. He looked over at Zara and nodded his head. She looked back at Luca, Jasper, and Freya.

"Fine." She sighed.

"We will be alright, mom." Luca walked over and gave Zara a hug, "I promise."

"As touching as this moment is," Axton interrupted, "it is now my time to depart. I will fill Kato in on everything." He turned and looked at Jasper, "I will see you tomorrow." Then he nodded to everyone.

The platform he was standing on began to flicker and shrink. Smoke started rolling into it. Then, just like that, it sent out a flash. When everyone refocused their eyes, Axton was gone. The bracelet was back on the floor in his place.

"Note to self." Jasper walked over and grabbed the bracelet, "That flash sucks."

Everyone laughed. Jasper slid the bracelet on as Zara composed herself. She no longer carried a sense of worry with her, now she meant business.

"If you guys are doing this, then you need to get your rest." She turned and looked at Freya and Jasper, "The couch and an air mattress are not going to give you the rest you will need." She looked at Freya, "You can come and sleep in my room with me." Then she looked at Luca, who nodded, and then she looked at Jasper, "You can sleep with Luca."

They all nodded, then retreated to their respective areas. Zara was right, the journey ahead of them was going to require rest. The next few days would involve a lot of walking and sleeping on the ground. Their bodies were not going to like them. For tonight though, they all climbed into their assigned spots in bed and tried to treat themselves to some well-deserved rest.

CHAPTER FIFTEEN

"Hey!" Luca shook the bed, causing Jasper to jump up, "Time to wake up." He laughed.

"So not funny." Jasper smirked as he sat up and stretched.

"Eh," Luca turned and continued digging through his closet, "I thought it was hilarious." He smiled as he turned back around and tossed two backpacks on his bed.

Jasper threw the rest of the covers off of him and climbed out of bed. Jasper was still waking up, and not fully alert, when he caught sight of himself in the mirror on Luca's wall.

"Where's my shirt?" Jasper looked at Luca, confused scratching at his head. Then crossed his arms around his chest, realizing he was shirtless.

"Yeah," Luca laughed, "I noticed you did that through the night at some point. Guess you had some type of wild dream." He smirked, "So, what was your dream about?" Luca batted his eyes playfully.

"Oh, shut it." Jasper laughed, "Just get packed." he threw one of the backpacks at Luca.

Both boys got dressed for the day, then packed their bags for the journey ahead of them. Jasper grabbed the necklace out of the box and slipped it into his backpack. He decided he would leave the box and journal put up safe in Luca's room, just as a cautionary move. Once they were finished packing, they headed downstairs to meet up with Freya and Zara.

"Good morning." Zara greeted the boys as they walked downstairs. "Everything packed and ready to go?" she tried to hide the worry and stress she was feeling.

"Yep." Jasper looked around the room, "Is Freya down yet?" he asked.

"Yeah," Zara pointed to the kitchen, "she's in the kitchen waiting for us to join her for a meal before you all head off." She looked at Jasper, "Why don't you go join her? I want to talk with Luca for a moment. We will be in shortly."

"Sure." Jasper nodded and headed to the kitchen, leaving Luca and Zara at the base of the stairs.

"Hey!" Freya smiled, patting the spot beside her, "Come sit."

"You're very peppy this morning." Jasper said as he entered the room.

"I think it's more nerves than anything." She confessed. Jasper knew that feeling all too well. He was used to going on trips to fetch things for his father, but this was different. He was going off somewhere he had never been before, somewhere no one had been since his mother hid it from the world. While Jasper didn't know his mom, he knew enough to tell from her writings that she wouldn't send him somewhere dangerous being unprepared. Even still, his nerves ate at him.

"I get it, but we'll be fine." He said as he joined Freya at the table.

"Jasper," Freya's smile faded away and was replaced by a more severe look, "why are you so sure everything is going to work out?"

"What do you mean?" He reached out and took Freya's hand, "Is everything okay?"

"It's just," she looked up at him, "you're so sure. What if your mother is actually someone bad? Or worse, what if she and your family are dead?" She looked back down, "I just don't know how you can stay so positive with it all."

Jasper thought for a moment. He was shocked to hear someone say that he was being positive. Sure he wasn't being negative, but he wasn't doing that well of a job at keeping his emotions in check either over the situation. Then he realized Freya hadn't seen those parts of him yet.

"I have not been positive throughout this entire experience." Jasper began to unload all of his current problems, "I have had my ups and downs. It's been a lot to take in. I've found out my past was a lie. I'm not from this world. I'm still not entirely sure what I am. My parents had to put me in hiding, but for what I have no idea. And the list goes on and on. I guess when it comes down to it, I have hope and trust. The Lady in White told me she feels that my family is still alive. I have no reason not to believe that." He squeezed her hand, "Even if it ends up being a sad story, I at least did everything I could to get back with my family. That's the best anyone can do in a circumstance like this. Just fight and do what needs to be done until you get back to them."

"So," Freya looked down and softly spoke, "you're saying you'd do whatever was necessary to get back to your family?"

"Isn't that what family is supposed to be? A group of people you'd do anything for, no matter the cost?" Jasper asked.

"I guess you're right." Freya softly smiled, looking back up at Jasper. "Thanks."

"I don't know what you're thanking me for." Jasper sat back in his chair, "It should be me thanking you and Luca for taking this journey with me."

"What's that?" Luca said as he and Zara entered the kitchen, "Do I hear gratitude being handed out?" He sat down at the table, "My turn, do me next." He chuckled.

They all laughed as Zara joined them at the table. Jasper looked around smiling, he was savoring this moment. For some reason, he felt like things were not going to be the same after this trip. Once he had the missing piece, things would change. He would be one step closer to finding his family. Hard telling what new information Luna would have, and there was still the looming attack from his vision. Jasper knew things would not be like this again for a while. So for now, he chose to cast out the worries and enjoy the moment he was being gifted with.

"I think the toughest part about the next few days is going to be not waking up to your breakfast." Luca said as he took the last bite off of his plate.

"Something tells me you'll survive." Jasper poked fun.

"I am going to be so worried about all of you." Zara chuckled softly, fighting back crying, "Anyways," she quickly forced a smile, "looks like you all are finished. We should get you on your way. I'm sure Kato wants to have words with you before you all head out." She directed that last part at Jasper.

Jasper nodded in reply. They all finished and cleaned up, then grabbed their bags. Zara used the basement door as the location for the portal. She hugged them all then sent them on their way.

"Be careful!" she called as the portal closed.

Jasper, Freya, and Luca exited the portal and walked into the Main Hall, where Axton and Kato were waiting for them.

"Hey, dad." Jasper said.

"Jasper." Kato's eyes gleamed at the sight of his son, "Axton has filled me in on all the details of what has happened," his gaze shifted to the group as a whole, "and what you three have to do." He looked at Luca, "Luca,

I thank you for agreeing to take this journey with Jasper. You heard the call to action, and you are taking it. Nothing could make us happier."

"Thank you." Luca appreciated Kato's kind words.

"I hear you are new," Kato looked at Freya, "and that you have ties to Jasper." He fought to hide his suspicions from coming to sight, "I am grateful he was able to find someone who could train him, and I thank you for taking this journey with him as well."

"Thank you, sir." Freya smiled, grabbing Jasper's hand.

"Finally," Kato turned and looked at Jasper, "my how much you've grown. You have taken what has come at you and allowed it to better you. I am so proud of the man you are becoming. I could not ask for a better son."

"Love you too, dad." Jasper, overwhelmed, rushed to Kato's side. He hadn't realized how much he missed his father until this moment. Jasper grabbed ahold of Kato and squeezed him tightly. He didn't want to let go. He knew reality would come crashing back once he did, but he also knew what was at stake. Jasper released Kato from his hold and rejoined Luca and Freya.

"So then," Kato composed himself, "do you guys have everything you need to head off?"

"Yeah, everything's packed. Mom made sure to go over a list with us before we left." Luca patted his bag.

"That sounds like Zara." Kato chuckled, "Very well, Axton will see you out. Good luck, be safe, and we will be waiting for your return." Then he walked off, heading to his office.

"Come with me." Axton waved his hand for the kids to follow him, leading them to the door.

"How are you feeling, Axton?" Jasper asked, "I noticed the memory block being broken seemed to do a number on you. Is everything alright?"

"Well, I've got a little bit of a headache, but I think that's due to old memories rushing forward. My energy feels a little lower than normal," Axton stopped and faced Jasper, "but don't worry about me. I just need to take it easy and recharge. I'll be fine."

"Good." Jasper took comfort in Axton's words, "I would hate to think that I did something to hurt you."

"You're good." Axton winked, "I've been around for a while. Something as simple as a memory spell is not going to be my downfall." Axton began walking again.

"How is dad doing?" Jasper followed.

"He's managing." Axton reassured, "I think he's trying to give you your space through all of this. You mean the world to him. I think he's just scared to lose you."

"He should know better than that." Jasper quickly replied, "He's my dad."

"What about when you find your real dad?" Freya chimed in, "I think that's what Axton is hinting at. He worries that when you find your family, it will erase him from the picture."

"Wait! What? Is that true?" Shocked, Jasper stopped Axton and asked.

"He's never voiced it, but I am sure it is on his mind." Axton replied softly.

"Yeah, but he's always going to be my dad." Jasper replied, "Tell him that for me, Axton. Let him know. It doesn't matter where this journey of mine ends, there will always be a place for him."

"I will." Axton nodded as he opened the door to let them out, "Be safe, and please do come back in one piece." He joked.

"Don't worry," Luca threw his arm around Jasper, "We'll keep him safe." He said as he ran his hand threw Jasper's hair to mess it up.

They all laughed, said goodbye to Axton, and headed off. Jasper guided them to Lyteshaed's exit. When they reached the gate, Jasper stopped and dug the necklace out of his bag and put it on.

"All of this fuss for a piece to a necklace." Freya stated.

"The things you do for family." Jasper laughed.

"Yeah, but what could be so special about it?" Luca asked, "Especially, to have to split it into pieces and hide them."

"I don't know." Jasper shrugged, "I'm hoping to find that out after we have this piece." He turned and looked at Luca and Freya, "Look, this is your last chance to back out. You don't have to make this trip with me."

"You're right, we don't." Freya said, "We want to."

"Yeah, we're here for you. We've got your back." Luca added.

"Well, then," Jasper smiled, "let's get going."

Luca and Freya followed Jasper as he led them south of Lyteshaed. The beginning of this trip would be familiar to Jasper. The field where he performed the ritual was this way. When they reached the field, his necklace began to glow.

"Look," Freya pointed out, "It's glowing."

"Who would have thought that this whole time," Jasper looked down at the necklace, "I was so close to a marker?"

Jasper slowly spun, watching the necklace to see which way caused it to glow brighter. The direction that caused it to glow the brightest led to an old, hidden away, path. Jasper had never seen it before, and he knew every inch of this field. The necklace must have caused the first layer of the shielding to fall, allowing for them to pass through.

"This way." He announced, walking towards the path.

"Jasper?" Freya called.

"Jasper, where are you?" Luca called after her.

Jasper turned around to see both Freya and Jasper looking directly at him.

"Funny, guys." He grinned, "Okay, enough joking. Come on."

Freya and Luca didn't budge, though. Jasper tried again, but still nothing. He walked to them.

"Guys, come on." He said.

"Where'd you go?" They both asked.

"You really couldn't see me? I was right in front of you." He pointed to the path, "Wait, can you guys not see the path?"

"No, all I see is woods." Freya said.

"Well yeah, but there's an opening with a trail right there." Jasper pointed again as if maybe this time they would see it.

"Nope." Luca shook his head, "I'm seeing what she is." Luca looked at the necklace, "It's the necklace. It's letting you see it, but not us."

"So, if we all want to pass, then we all have to be touching the necklace?" Freya asked.

"It would make sense. Yet, another way to ensure it was Jasper that found the piece, and no one else." Luca pointed out.

"There's only one way to find out." Jasper took the necklace off, "Here, come touch it."

Freya and Luca walked up to Jasper, and each touched a piece of the necklace. Jasper looked at them as they both widened their eyes.

"You see it now." He smiled, enjoying their looks of amazement.

They both shook their heads, looking at the new open path in front of them. It was just an ordinary trail cut through the trees, nothing special. The fact that it wasn't there a moment ago was what had them shocked and slightly excited.

"Okay, let's go." Jasper said.

They all three walked, side by side, together and entered the trail. Once they were on the trail, Luca and Freya let go of the necklace.

"You guys are still with me, right?" Jasper asked.

"Yeah." Luca responded as he looked around, examining the new area.

"So as long as we all touch the necklace at each marker, we can all enter to the next area. It must shield back once we pass. Since we've done entered, we don't have to keep ahold of the necklace." Jasper explained.

"Sounds right to me." Freya replied, as she too took in the area.

"Well, come on then." Jasper put the necklace back on, "Let's get moving."

"Bossy, isn't he?" Luca teased to Freya.

"Yes, quite." She giggled.

"I'll leave you both at the next marker." Jasper grinned as he began walking off, leaving Luca and Freya rushing to catch up with him.

The day continued, repeating the same pattern. Every time the necklace began to glow, Jasper would search for the next marker. Once he found it, they would all three grab the necklace and continue forward. The trip was going smoothly. Jasper knew that Zara, and everyone else, was overreacting by worrying about them. This was a simple retrieval mission. Then Freya froze, and everything changed.

"Freya?" Jasper walked up to her, "What's the matter?"

"She's close." Freya had tears in her eyes as she spoke.

"Who's close?" Luca asked.

"Camille." Freya answered.

"How is that possible?" Jasper asked.

"We've got to get to cover." Luca declared, scanning the area for anything out of the ordinary.

"Come on, Freya, we have to go." Jasper urged her.

Freya wouldn't move, though. Jasper kept trying to make her follow, but she stood there frozen staring off in front of her. Jasper turned around to see what had her attention, and that was when he saw her.

She wore a black, skin-tight, top with leather pants, which were split down the sides in a pattern. She had on some type of combat boots. Her hair was long, dark brown fading into a deep red. She had her hair ponytailed and braided, laying down and around her shoulder. Her eyes were glowing a deep blood red. She stared straight at Jasper as she walked towards the group. Jasper couldn't help but notice how graceful she walked. He expected something menacing, but she carried herself with a terrifying elegance.

"Well, well, well." She said as she approached them, "What do we have here?" She looked at Freya, then the two boys, "Looks like little Freya has gotten herself some friends."

"Leave her alone." Jasper stood in front of Freya.

"Oh, little boy." Camille grinned, "What could you possibly do to stop me?"

"There's a lot that I'm capable of, Camille." Jasper began charging his energy, his eyes started glowing a dark blue.

"I see she told you about me." Camille smirked, as she played with the dagger she held in her hands.

Jasper continued charging his energy. He began to bring it out but was interrupted.

"Jasper, stop!" Luca shouted. "It's a trap?"

"Well," Camille laughed, "aren't you smarter than you look." She stared Luca down, "Looks and brains, such a keeper."

"What do you mean, a trap?" Jasper asked.

"She's not really here." Luca explained, kicking dirt at her which flew right through her, "She's somehow project-ing herself here. She wants to see what you're capable of. Don't show her."

Jasper calmed down, realizing Luca was right. Still, he wondered how she was able to get through the shielding his mother had placed. He also wanted to know what she wanted with him and Freya.

"Well, isn't that a bummer." She faked a frown, "Oh well." She sighed, "There's always next time." Then with a grin, she threw the dagger straight at Freya.

The boys both turned and knocked Freya down to the ground with them, the dagger faded away as it kept flying. Sure Camille was just a projection, but there was no sense in assuming she couldn't still hurt them. They all stood back up.

"Where did she go?" Jasper asked, scanning the area. There was no sign of Camille.

"I don't know." Luca did the same, "She's gone."

"Guys, I think we should keep going." Freya, no longer frozen in fear, spoke. "That was too close for comfort. I don't know about you two, but I'd like to get as far away from this area as possible."

They all nodded and continued walking. Jasper kept going over the events in his head, though. He wondered why she went through the process of projecting herself here, instead of tracking them down herself. Why did she want to know what Jasper was capable of? Eventually, the sun began setting, and the moon started to rise. This brought on a new question. Where would they set up camp?

"This looks as good a spot as any to stop for the night." Luca spoke up.

"Are you sure we will be okay to stop and camp here?" Freya asked, still frightened from the encounter with Camille.

"I think so." Luca looked at Jasper, "What do you think?"

"I think Luca's right. Besides, we've passed a few more markers since the encounter. She was only able to project herself, she couldn't enter. I doubt she could project herself in this far." He attempted to reassure Freya.

"If you say so." She scanned the area, "I still think we should put up some sigils just to be safe." Luca and Jasper agreed with her. They all made a circle, then each of them put down a sigil to protect them.

"There." Jasper said as they all finished, "Now we have a

shield of our own within many shields set by my mother."

"I think I'm just going to be on guard until we return to safety." Freya explained.

"We will be fine." Luca tried to comfort her, "You should lay down. We all need our rest."

"He's right. We should reach the cave tomorrow, as long as we don't run into any more trouble. The sooner we get the piece, the sooner we can go back to Lyteshaed." Jasper reassured her once again.

"Okay, you're right." Freya sighed, trying to release her fear.

They all laid their sleeping bags around the fire that Luca had made. Jasper laid there under the night sky. It had been a while since he had been able to just lie under the stars and look up at them. The stars and the ocean, those were always the two things able to calm Jasper down. Once his thoughts slowed down, he looked at both Luca and Freya. How were both of them already asleep? Jasper laid there watching the night sky as the stars twinkled above. Until he too joined them in sleep.

CHAPTER SIXTEEN

Jasper woke up as the sun was beginning to rise. He saw bright hues of pink and orange streaking through the sky, with tints of a deep purple mixed throughout. He took a deep breath and stretched as he rolled over to begin waking up the others. That was when he noticed it.

"Luca?" he whispered, "Luca!" he whispered louder.

"Hm?" Luca groggily rolled over, trying to keep sleeping.

"Luca, wake up." Jasper moved over to Luca and nudged him awake.

"What?" Luca, in his still tired state, snapped.

"Freya's gone." Jasper pointed to her empty sleeping bag.

"What?" Luca, becoming more alert, sat up.

"She's gone. There's no way something could have gotten in here, right? Plus, she was too scared to try and split from the group. What could have happened?" Jasper began panicking.

"Calm down." Luca stood up, "Let's search the area. I'm sure she's fine."

Jasper nodded, then they both began searching the area. Her bag was still here, so that must be a good sign. Jasper tried to figure out what could have happened. They had their sigils up, so no one threatening should have been able to pass. As they continued examining the area, they also canceled out the sigils.

"I don't get it." Jasper spoke up, "There's nowhere she could have gone. What if she's in trouble? Or worse, what if Camille somehow found a way to get her?"

"Shh." Luca silenced Jasper and pointed behind him, "Listen, I hear something."

Jasper backed up to Luca. They both stood silently listening. Then Jasper heard it too, sticks snapping. The sound was getting closer, it sounded like it was coming from only one source. At least the odds were in their favor. Jasper wondered if someone took off with Freya, and now they were coming back to finish the job. The figure emerged from the clearing stepping into the opening. Without hesitation, the boys charged.

"Whoa there!" Freya shouted, "It's me."

"Freya!" Jasper and Luca halted in their tracks, "We were worried something happened to you." Jasper rushed to her side.

"One of us more than the other." Luca teased, "I told him it was probably nothing."

"Well, thanks for the worry, but seriously I'm fine." She smiled, walking to gather her things and clean up her area.

"Where were you?" Jasper asked, still not entirely sure she was okay.

"Well, Jasper." she laughed, "If you must know, I had to use the bathroom." She turned to face him as she stuffed a roll of toilet paper into her bag.

"Oh." Jasper blushed. "Gotcha."

"That's great." Luca busted out laughing.

"Oh, of course," Jasper shot him a glare, "laugh away." He walked over and picked up his bag, "Come on, we still got a long walk ahead of us."

Freya grinned and headed off behind Jasper. Luca, still snickering, threw the rest of his stuff in his bag. He made sure everything was picked up. Then he rushed off, catching up with the others.

"Wait for me." He called out with a laugh.

They continued on the path, stopping as the necklace began to glow and following the pattern they had been. The closer they got to the cave, the more Jasper began to sense it.

"We're getting close." Jasper told the others.

"Are you sure?" Luca asked.

"How do you know?" Freya asked.

"I don't know. I feel it." Jasper explained, "It's like I can feel something pulling at me, calling to me."

"Maybe you sense your mother's energy?" Luca pondered.

"That could be." Freya said, "After all, this was all done for you. She is your mom. It would make sense that you would be able to pick up on her energy signature. The place that this missing piece is held is most likely dripping with traces of her energy."

"I don't know what it is. All I know is that we are really close." Jasper continued walking, almost as if he was in a trance.

They all continued forward. The necklace began glowing brighter than it had for any marker during the entire journey. Jasper didn't acknowledge it, though. He just kept walking, following the pull. Luca and Freya looked at one another and continued behind him. Then Jasper pulled back a branch, stepped out of the trail, and froze. Freya and Luca exited the path and stood beside him. They all stood still.

"We found it." Jasper said, staring at the entrance to the cave.

"You okay?" Luca turned and looked at Jasper.

Jasper nodded and started walking towards the cave.

"Hold on!" Freya called out, grabbing Jasper's arm, "We should be careful. You need to be alert. There could be traps protecting the cave."

"You're right." Jasper nodded, snapping out of his trance-like state, "Sorry." He looked at Freya and Luca, "It's just so surreal."

"We get it." Freya smiled.

"Yeah, but we need to go about this slowly." Luca explained.

Jasper agreed with them. They all then decided the best plan was to not rush. They would take it slow and search for potential traps as they go. On the chance there were any last-minute traps put in place by his mother, they would then retreat back and plan from there.

Once they were all in agreement, Jasper led them to the cave entrance. Jasper took a breath and then entered the cave, disappearing, leaving Freya and Luca standing cluelessly behind.

"So," Luca shrugged and looked at Freya, "I guess there was one last marker."

"You think." She glanced over, rolling her eyes at him. "Jasper," she called, "We're not with you. You need to let us in."

They stood there waiting, but Jasper didn't come out. They looked at each other, panic beginning to rise.

"Jasper, this isn't funny." Luca stated, "You need to let us in now."

"Jasper, come on." Freya added.

Then Jasper's head popped back out, his face was ecstatic. He brought his hand out, holding the necklace for them to touch and enter.

"You guys need to see this." He said, pulling his head back into the cave but still holding his hand out.

Freya and Luca looked at each other, wondering what they were about to see. They both reached out and took the necklace and entered the cave. They froze right beside Jasper, all three of them standing in amazement at what they were seeing.

The outside of the cave looked exactly like you would expect any old cave to look like. It seemed damp and earthy, rocks everywhere. From the outside, one would assume they were in for a dim, if not dark, walk in a spooky cave, that was sure to house bats, bugs, spiders, and other creepy crawlies. What they walked into was not the case, it was not the case at all.

It was as if they had entered into a giant geode that had just been cracked open. There were blues, purples, and pinks everywhere. Crystals covered the entire cave's walls and ceiling. There were clear crystals placed every so often mixed in with the colored ones. They seemed to house some type of light source that refracted off all the colors, lighting the cave. Underneath them was a transparent floor, with the cleanest water any of them had ever seen running below it.

"What is this place?" Luca asked, "I've never seen a cave like this."

"Is the floor made out of clear quartz?" Freya asked, bending down to peak through and watch the water run.

"I don't know," Jasper shrugged as he examined it closer, "but I think it is."

"This place is beautiful." Freya replied.

"It is." Jasper agreed, "Come on, let's keep going."

Luca and Freya nodded and followed Jasper. It didn't take long for them to have to stop again. Jasper spotted a pillar in the distance, it had something floating atop it.

"That must be it." Freya gasped.

"Come on." Jasper rushed off.

"I'm kind of surprised it was this simple." Luca laughed as he and Freya ran behind Jasper.

"Whoa!" Jasper halted in his tracks.

"Yeah," Freya said as she and Luca stopped beside him, "that is if you don't count the bottomless pit surrounding the pillar with the floating item on it." She spoke sarcastically, turning her head and shaking it at Luca.

"Well, yeah." He replied, "There's that tiny detail." He peered over the edge, watching the water underneath them flow into the pit.

There was no way to tell how deep the pit was, or if there even was a bottom. Jasper stood there, thinking. There was no way he was put through everything to just be stuck. Then it hit him, everything he was put through. His mom was training him for this moment.

"Guys," Jasper placed a hand on Luca and Freya's shoulders, "I know what I have to do."

"You really have a plan to cross this?" Luca gestured to the pit as if Jasper did not see it.

"I do." Jasper smiled, "My mother made sure I was trained for it." He looked at Freya, "You two need to back away and give me space to do this."

Freya and Luca took a few steps back to give Jasper an area for him to pull off whatever he was about to do. Jasper began to charge his energy and then brought it out. He let it pour out of his hands to the edge of the cliff, forming a circular platform. Once he felt like it was stable enough, he stepped on.

As he concentrated on keeping the energy constant, he willed it to move. He used this energy platform to carry him across the pit and to the pillar where the item was floating. As he got closer, his heart began beating faster. He could make the piece out better now, it was thin and looked like a ring. As he examined more, he saw that it seemed to be about the size of the hole in the necklace. He also saw that it had its edges flared out and small circles punctured all around it. He figured it must slide right over the jewels and seal itself in the empty circle. He also noticed it was very clear that something would still fit into it too. This wasn't the only piece missing from the necklace. Jasper reached out for the silver piece. As he closed his hands around it, his energy jolted back into him. He had let his mind quit focusing on his energy, and now he was falling because of it.

"Jasper!" Luca yelled.

"No!" Freya shouted.

Pink energy streamed out of Freya, flying out to catch Jasper. When she had ahold of him, she slowly pulled him in. She set him down carefully on the cliff's edge. Freya and Luca rushed to Jasper to make sure he was okay. Jasper laid on the ground, heart racing, trying to catch his breath from the panic that had set in within him.

"Jasper!" Freya called out, nudging in front of Luca.

Luca backed away. Freya grabbed Jasper's head and lifted him up.

"Are you okay?" She asked, pushing his hair out of his

face. "I thought I lost you."

"I'm okay." Jasper nodded, still catching his breath.

Freya's eyes were full of tears. She let a smile form across her face. She pulled Jasper in and hugged him tightly. Jasper, thankful for Freya, squeezed her closer to him. As they sat there, Jasper felt Freya lean back. He lifted his head to look at her, she was still emotional. Jasper stared at Freya while Freya stared at him. Then in the moment, Freya leaned in and began to kiss him.

As she began to pull away, Jasper pulled her back in to continue the kiss she had started. Jasper was overwhelmed with emotions. He had a missing piece to the necklace, he was going to find out more about his family, he had his friend by his side, and now he had the girl. His life was becoming whole again.

"Thanks for saving me." Jasper grinned, pulling his head back, "I don't know what I would have done, had you not been here."

"Don't mention it." Freya nuzzled her head on Jasper's shoulder as she slid her finger on his chest, "You would have done the same for me." She said as she helped Jasper up, "So, did you get it? Can I see it?"

"I did." Jasper handed her the piece.

"Jasper, don't!" Luca shouted, rushing to Jasper, but it was too late.

"What?" Jasper looked at Luca, puzzled.

"I'm sorry, Jasper." Freya closed her hand and backed away from Jasper.

"Freya? What's going on? I don't understand." Jasper stood there, confused.

"She's been working against us this whole time." Luca accused. "Haven't you?" He spat with venom.

"Somebody, tell me what's going on." Jasper demanded.

"She's been working against us this entire time. I wasn't sure at first, but now I am." Luca explained as Jasper stood there becoming mortified. "The final sign was just now. She just did something she has overly advertised she could not do." He looked at Jasper, "She saved you by sending out her energy. She knew how to do it this whole time. That means all the times you trained, she was purposely dragging it out." He looked back at Freya, "Of course, this wasn't the first time she did it either."

"What do you mean?" Jasper looked at Luca.

"How do you think Camille was able to appear here? She almost had me. I thought she wasn't moving because she was frozen in fear. That wasn't the case, though, was it? No, she was the one projecting her."

"Freya?" Jasper shot his head to her, "Tell me it's not true."

"You don't understand," Freya looked away, shamefully, avoiding eye contact with Jasper, "I had to."

"I don't understand?" Jasper's stomach dropped as he questioned her, his shock turning to anger. "Why don't you enlighten me then?"

"I'm sorry, Jasper." A tear fell down Freya's cheek, "There was no other choice for me. She has my family."

Freya then lifted her hand and slid her finger through the air, creating a portal out of thin air.

Jasper and Luca gasped as the portal formed and then jumped back when someone began to step out.

"So, we meet again." Camille smiled victoriously, stepping out of the portal.

Camille stood there beside Freya, smirking at Jasper. She wore a black dress that hugged her body and black high heels. Her hair was no longer in a braid, now it freely flowed straight down. She also had some type of black headband that shined when the light touched it. Her eyes were light brown with yellow streaking. They were no longer charged with her red energy like they had been before.

"Stay back!" Luca shouted as he jumped in front of Jasper.

"Oh, silly boy." Camille chuckled, "I don't want him." She glared at Jasper, "I got what I came for right here." She held her hand out at Freya.

"Jasper, I'm so sorry." Freya continued apologizing.

"Really, dear." Camille shook her head, disapprovingly, "This is so unbecoming."

"I've done what you want, Camille." Freya clenched the necklace piece in her hand, "Now give me back my family, or you can say goodbye to this piece."

"Oh?" Camille grinned out of the corner of her lips, showing her teeth, "She has threats." Camille walked in front of Freya as if she was walking on a runaway, "That makes this moment *so* much sweeter."

"What are you going on about?" Freya stood her ground, "Give me my family back."

"Child," Camille laughed gracefully, "I've never had your family. They left you behind long ago."

"No." Freya trembled, "You're lying!"

"No," Camille turned, waving her finger at Freya, "I *was* lying. *Now*, I'm telling the truth." She turned to the boys, teasing Freya, "You'd think she would have drawn the conclusion long ago," Camille faced Freya, "I'm bad."

"If you know what's good for you, you'll both leave now!" Luca shouted.

"Feisty." Camille looked Luca up and down, "I like it." She then turned and looked at Freya, "But he is right, our time is up here. We leave now." She walked towards the portal that still lay open, "Come on, dear."

"No!" Freya backed away from Camille. "I have no reason to go with you. You've lied to me, you betrayed me, and you used me."

"Darling, I'm evil. What did you expect?" Camille held out her hand, "Now come on."

"I said no." Freya replied.

"You're really testing my patience right now." Camille walked up to Freya, "Where do you suppose you'll go?" she pointed to Luca and Jasper, "Do you really think they will accept you back after what you've done?"

"Jasper? Luca?" Freya turned and looked at both boys.

Luca continued his stern glare, staring down both Freya and Camille. Jasper stood behind him, defeated, still trying to make sense of everything.

"Now," Camille grabbed Freya's arm, "I said come on." dragging her to the portal.

"Jasper, please!" Freya called out, "I'm sorry!"

Luca didn't budge. Jasper looked down at the ground, trying to drown out the cries from Freya. She had betrayed him. She knew how much this meant to him. That it was the only way to find his family. She worked against them every step of the way. A tear ran down Jasper's cheek as he turned his back to her.

"Jasper!" Freya shouted one last time reaching her hand out as Camille pulled her in, the portal closing behind them.

CHAPTER SEVENTEEN

Luca turned around to face Jasper. Jasper stood there, emotionless. He felt empty. In one quick flash, he lost everything. He went from feeling like he finally had it all, to finding out it was all a rouse and he truly had nothing to begin with. Luca hugged him.

"Jasper," Luca said, holding him tightly, "I'm so sorry."

Jasper didn't move, he didn't respond. He just stood there with Luca hugging him, not knowing how he was going to react. Then it all kicked in, he began to boil over. He was about to blow, and he knew there was no avoiding it. Jasper shook himself loose, out of Luca's hold. Luca backed away.

"Are you okay?" He tried to walk closer to Jasper, but Jasper pulled away again. "Hey?"

Jasper could tell he was hurting Luca by acting this way, but he was fighting not lashing out. Luca, however, did not care and kept trying to break down Jasper's wall.

"We will find a way to fix this. I promise." Luca reached his hand out to Jasper.

"Stop!" Jasper shouted, causing Luca to jump.

"I'm sorry." Luca slid his hand through his dark hair, then stuck it in his pocket. "I'm just trying to be supportive."

"Supportive?" Jasper laughed, "You're probably dying on the inside to tell me you told me so. You've not liked Freya since day one. That was never a secret." Jasper spat, "Go ahead, say it!" he shouted.

"Jasper?" Luca gasped. It was clear he was hurt.

"No, it's true." Jasper turned from Luca, "What? Were you so jealous that if she had all of my attention, we wouldn't be friends anymore? What was it?" Jasper turned back, glaring at Luca.

"You seriously cannot be blaming me for this?" Luca placed a hand on his chest and let out a shocked laugh.

Jasper didn't reply. He just stood there, realizing what he had just said. On the inside, he was hurting. He knew he didn't really blame Luca, but he also knew there was no taking back what he had done said.

"Wow!" Luca scoffed, throwing his hands in the air, "Can you really be that oblivious?" He walked off, then turned around and walked straight up to Jasper. "You can hide behind whatever emotion you want to, but I'm done. You know how I feel about you. There's no way I would ever hurt you. I just traveled all this way to help you." Luca was getting more heated. "I can't continue doing this if this is how you're going to be. I thought you were better than this." He turned his back to Jasper and walked away.

"Luca." Jasper reached out his arm as Luca walked away, "Luca, I'm sorry. I just got angry and lashed out, I didn't mean it. I-"

"I don't want to hear it right now." Luca interrupted him, his voice beginning to break. "Just take me home, okay?"

Jasper could hear Luca begin to sniffle. Jasper felt crushed, watching Luca as he walked over to stand in the corner. He knew he enjoyed Luca's company. He never realized how much Luca meant to him, though. He had also never understood how much he meant to Luca. Jasper felt horrible for being so blind, to himself and to Luca. He wondered if he could fix what he had done. He would begin by following Luca's request.

Jasper walked to the cave's entrance, Luca following behind, and drew a sigil on the wall to open a portal to Zara's house. The portal opened, and Jasper stepped to the side. He wanted to grab Luca, to hug him, to fix it all, but he saw how Luca looked and decided to let him be. Once Luca walked through, Jasper followed.

Zara had seen the portal open, so she was standing by waiting to congratulate everyone. She was confused to see only Luca and Jasper walk through. Her confusement changed to concern when she registered the way both boys looked.

"What happened? Where's Freya?" She rushed to their aid.

"Not now, mom." Luca looked down and stood away from Jasper, "I just need to go to my room." His voice breaking more, "Okay?"

"Luca." Jasper tried again, but Luca ignored him walking to the stairs.

"Okay." Zara shifted into mother mode and looked at Jasper, "What is going on? Where is Freya? Where is the piece? What is wrong with Luca?" She grilled.

Jasper explained how the trip went, telling her about the projection of Camille showing up. He then told her about the cave and how he got the piece. He told her about falling and Freya catching him. Zara's eyes rose when she heard that part. Jasper explained how Luca made the same realization before Jasper could. He told her how Freya took the piece and brought Camille to them and what went down. Then lastly, he told Zara how he had gone off on Luca. He also apologized and explained how he wished he could take it back. That he realized how much Luca meant to him, and he didn't want to lose him too.

"I see." Zara took everything in patiently, "Sounds like there is a lot to discuss. A meeting with your father and the Elders needs to be set up at once." She looked upstairs, "For now, I need to go be a mother and check on my son."

"I understand." Jasper looked down.

"Jasper," Zara reached for Jasper's chin and lifted his head up, "I'm not mad at you."

"Thanks," Jasper, still broken, replied, "but I'm sure Luca will never want to talk to me again."

"Oh, nonsense." She smiled lovingly, "You guys had a fight, it happens. Luca is hurt right now, but I see how you boys are with each other. He will forgive you, I promise." She gave Jasper a hug then went upstairs to check on Luca.

Jasper went to the living room and sat on the couch. He had so much on his mind. He had to figure out how to get the necklace piece back. He also had to prepare for whatever tricks Camille had up her sleeves. More importantly, he had to fix what he had just done to Luca. Jasper let his mind drift in thought. Not realizing how tired and worn out he was, Jasper fell into a deep sleep.

Jasper entered into the dream realm, standing in his field. He wondered if Luna was asleep. He had never knowingly called for her, but now was a good time to try. Jasper concentrated on bringing Luna into his realm. As he focused, he began to sense her presence. He opened his eyes, a flare of light shot down from the sky, and out stepped Luna.

"Jasper?" Luna asked as she stepped through the light, "What's going on?"

"We have a problem." Jasper looked down, "Camille got the piece from us."

"What?" Luna gasped, "How is this possible?"

"We had an enemy in our midst." He replied

"Who?" she asked.

"Freya." Jasper answered shamefully, "She was working against us the entire time."

"Why would she do this?" Luna asked, puzzled.

"She claims that Camille had her family and she was forced to, but..." Jasper paused, "I don't know that I can believe her."

"Where is she now?" Luna approached Jasper.

"She's with Camille. Freya portaled Camille to us. Then when Camille left, she pulled Freya into the portal with her."

"You mean you were face to face with Camille?" Luna asked.

"Yes." Jasper replied.

"And she didn't harm you?" Luna was confused. "This is oddly interesting."

"What do you mean?" Jasper was now the one puzzled.

"It's just, it doesn't fit the stories. This malevolent force had you in her grasps and then let you go? Why would she do this?" Luna examined Jasper. "I wonder…" Luna's voice trailed off.

"Luna," Jasper interrupted her thinking, "is there anything you have remembered that could be helpful? We need to get that piece back."

"I'm sorry, Jasper, but no. I told you my knowledge is tied to how much you unlock. Somehow the necklace was going to allow you to understand more. Until you get that piece, we are at a standstill." She then gasped, "Maybe, just maybe, that is why Camille did not harm you. She is most likely aware of the memory block by now. If she were to harm you, then she would be ending her chances of removing it. Still, she is someone to keep an eye on. At any time, she could strike at those closest to you. If anything, just to make her point."

"What would her point be?" Jasper asked.

"Who knows?" Luna shook her head, "It could be as simple as retaliating due to the memory block. A more worrisome reason could be that she knows more than we do. That she's just attempting to stop us from finding out more."

"You mean she could know who my family is?" Jasper jumped at any chance to find his family.

"It's possible." Luna replied.

"I want to be excited, but it also concerns me." Jasper replied, "I just wish that you were able to know more." He turned and looked at Luna, who was frozen in fear, "Luna, what's wrong?"

"Jasper," she stood there frozen, slowly speaking, "That attack… It's happening."

"What? When?" Jasper began to panic.

"Now." Luna looked at Jasper, her eyes widened.

Jasper jumped up off the couch. Zara walked into the room and saw this. She rushed to his side.

"Jasper, is everything okay?" she asked.

"No, nothing is okay." He replied, his mind racing.

"We will get the piece back, don't worry." Zara tried to calm Jasper.

"No, Zara. It's not about the necklace." Jasper explained, "Lyteshaed, it's under attack."

"What?" Zara took off.

Jasper followed behind her. Zara ran to a doorway, she began working on the sigil to open a portal to Lyteshaed. When she was done, she stood back in shock.

"Nothing is happening." Jasper stated.

"This is not good." Zara spoke, her eyes locked on the empty space where a portal should be.

"Why didn't the portal open?" Jasper asked, "You drew the sigil correctly."

"It's a failsafe." She turned and looked at Jasper, "If Lyteshaed is ever under attack, the portals are locked down. It is a way to save as many members as possible."

"So, what does this mean? How do we help them?" Jasper's panic began to rise again.

"I have to get to the Elders. There is a way to get around the failsafe, but they will all have to agree to use it." Zara explained, but her face made it seem like it was doubtful, "I must tell you, there is a high chance they will say no. Especially since we know what is happening because of your visions."

"No!" Jasper dropped to the ground, "There has to be a way to get there. We have to save them!" he exclaimed, closing his eyes.

"Jasper, it's the only way. There is no-" Zara froze.

Jasper opened his eyes to see energy flowing from his body into a portal swirling in the middle of Zara's floor. He jumped back.

"Did I do that?" He asked.

"Yes." Zara nodded, "What is it?" She asked.

"I think it's a way to Lyteshaed." Jasper reasoned.

"How can you be sure?" Zara worriedly examined the portal.

"That's what I was focusing on. I wanted there to be a way to get there." Jasper looked at the portal, "Now I have one."

"Let me go get Luca." Zara snapped out of her shocked state, "We are going to need help."

"I can't wait. I have to go now." Jasper looked at Zara then back into the portal, "It will stay open. Go get Luca and come help. I have to go save dad!"

"Jasper, wait!" Zara shouted, but it was too late. Jasper had done jumped into the portal.

Zara ran upstairs to get Luca. They had to hurry. If this was the attack Jasper had for seen, then it was going to take something special to save them. What they needed was a miracle.

CHAPTER EIGHTEEN

Jasper ran out of the portal. It had taken him to the field outside of Lyteshaed, where he performs the annual Ritual of Protection. The vision had come full circle. He had been brought back to where it all began. Without a moment's thought, Jasper took off running to the clan hall.

Everything was so familiar, it was like a nightmare come true. He could hear the screams, see the explosions. It was all so overwhelming. Jasper fought past his emotions and kept running. He was closing in on the wall.

Jasper rounded the wall and came upon the main grounds. Just like in his vision, there were piles of ashes lying everywhere. Jasper continued running, he saw the castle was ablaze. He worried about Axton. He didn't know what would happen to Axton if the entire castle crumbled down. Then Jasper had a flash of his dad fighting the hooded figure and took off running.

There they were both fighting, the hooded figure and Kato. While everything from the vision was coming true, Jasper couldn't help but notice that something felt different. Kato turned and caught Jasper running around the corner.

"Jasper! What are you doing here?" Kato yelled.

Kato threw an energy blast at the hooded figure, who easily deflected it away and laughed. Then, just as Jasper had already foreseen, they began to manifest a fireball above their head. Knowing what he now knew, Jasper knew this being had to be someone like him. No average person would be able to do something like this, but who could it be? Jasper figured if it were Camille, then she wouldn't have bothered with a hood. So who was it?

"Jasper, run!" Kato shouted.

"No, stop!" The hooded figure threw the fireball.

Jasper just froze. Even knowing what was going to happen, the fear still paralyzed him. Jasper braced himself. He could not believe this was how it was all going to end.

"Oh, no you don't!" A voice shouted, knocking Jasper to the ground.

Jasper, and whoever knocked him down, went rolling. Once they stopped, Jasper opened his eyes. He was shocked, and relieved, to see that it was Luca who was on top of him. Luca had just saved him.

"Luca?" Jasper groaned, his body had taken quite the impact.

"Did you really think I would give up on you that easy?" Luca smiled, staring into Jasper's eyes. "You're going to have to try harder than that to shake me off."

"I see this is beginning to become a trend." Jasper coughed up a laugh.

Luca remained silent, a grin forming as he continued looking down at Jasper. Jasper looked into his eyes. There was no longer hurt registering in them, but there was something else. Luca began to lower his body against Jasper's. Jasper tensed, at first, as Luca's body lightly pressed against his. He could tell Luca noticed but that he didn't mind. Luca bit his lip as he bent his head down and then pressed them against Jasper's. At first, Jasper jumped, but then he closed his eyes and gave in to what was happening.

Jasper felt the heat radiating from his and Luca's bodies as they pressed against each other. Pieces of Luca's hair brushed against his face. He felt the rapid beating of a heart, not knowing if it was his, Luca's, or a mixture of both in unison. Jasper began to lift his arms when Luca lifted his head up.

"I told you, you're stuck with me." Luca smiled, looking down at a wide-eyed Jasper.

Jasper's head rushed, his emotions went crazy. It took everything he had to keep himself lying still. He wondered where he and Luca went from here. Then his thoughts were interrupted by the hooded figure shouting and screaming. Jasper and Luca turned their heads to watch as they sent out an energy blast, then fell to the ground.

Luca jumped up, allowing Jasper to do the same. When they both turned to face the mystery attacker, they were shocked at what they saw. It was Freya. When she fell, the hood flipped back and revealed her face.

"Something doesn't seem right." Jasper said. He looked at Freya, who was on the ground squirming around and yelling.

"I agree." Luca replied, "This doesn't make any sense."

"That's not her energy around her." Jasper pointed to the almost blood-red energy swarming around her, "This has Camille all over it." Jasper looked around, "Wait, where's my dad?"

Jasper scanned the area and finally found Kato. He had been flung back into some debris. He was lying on the ground and wasn't moving. Jasper rushed to his side.

"Dad!" Jasper exclaimed, "Dad, wake up." He shoved on Kato, trying to wake him up.

"Jasper?" Kato's voice was raspy and fading, "Oh, Jasper, I'm glad you're safe." He reached his hand up to Jasper.

"I'm here." Jasper took Kato's hand and placed it on his face, holding his hand against Kato's so it wouldn't fall. "You're going to be fine. We're going to get you help."

"Jasper," Kato coughed, "I am so proud of the man you are becoming. You have given my life on this earth a purpose. For that, I am grateful." Kato smiled weakly.

"Dad, don't talk like this. You're going to be fine." Jasper repeated as tears began to fill his eyes.

"Did you defeat whoever attacked us?" Kato asked, trying to move his head to look around.

"No." Jasper shook his head, "It's Freya, but she is under

Camille's influence." Jasper nodded his head in Freya's direction, "She seems to be fighting it. Hopefully, she can. If she can't, we will do what is needed to save the clan." Jasper smiled down at Kato. "I'm the one who is lucky to get to call you dad."

Kato was fading quickly. Jasper fought back the tears filling his eyes. Luca silently kneeled beside Jasper, placing his hand on Jasper's shoulder. Jasper closed his eyes, he wasn't ready to let his father go. This wasn't fair.

"Make him remember." A female voice whispered.

"Who said that?" Jasper opened his eyes and looked around.

"Said what?" Luca asked, looking at Jasper puzzled.

"Jasper," The voice whispered again, "make him remember."

"I can't." Jasper was close to his breaking point.

"Can't what?" Luca was getting concerned.

"You've always been able to, Jasper. You just need to believe. The power is inside of you, my son." The voice faded away.

"Mom?" Jasper's heart dropped, realizing his mother was contacting him.

"Jasper, are you okay?" Luca looked at him.

Jasper closed his eyes. He had to focus on making Kato remember. He had no idea what Kato needed to remember. But if his mother was able to contact him about it, then it had to be important. Jasper concentrated and chanted in his head. Nothing happened.

"I'm sorry, dad, I can't do it. I can't make you remember." Jasper grabbed Kato close to him and held him.

A tear slid out of Jasper's eye. It slowly passed down his cheek, tracing his nose line, and then his lips. The teardrop fell from his chin and landed on Kato's forehead.

"Jasper." Luca gasped, nudging him. "Jasper, look."

He opened his eyes to see his teardrop rippling into Kato's skin. Kato absorbed the energy from his tear. As it faded, he began crying more intensely. It was no longer just a sad cry, Jasper was happy.

"Are you okay?" Luca looked at Jasper, who was looking down at Kato.

"Luca," Jasper laughed, his tears falling down, "he's my dad. My real dad."

"My son," Kato opened his eyes, his too were filled with tears, "you found me." He smiled, reaching up and placing his hand on Jasper's chest, "I will always be with you." His eyes began to close, "I love you." Kato's face softened as his hand dropped to the ground.

Jasper fell apart, holding Kato in his arms. His biological father and the father he had known had been one and the same this entire time. Then just as he found him, he lost him. This could not be the end. Jasper's attention got drawn to a screaming Freya.

"Jasper," she wept as she broke free from Camille's influence, the red energy dispersing, "I didn't mean for any of this to happen." She looked up at Jasper, "I will fix this, I promise." Freya began charging her energy, her body radiating vibrant pink waves, "I'll bring them back. I'll bring them all back." She looked at Jasper one last time and smiled, "Remember me." She whispered.

There was a flash. Jasper and Luca huddled over Kato's body, not knowing what was happening. When their vision came back, they were shocked at what they saw.

"Jasper, look." Luca tapped Jasper's arm.

Jasper looked around the clan grounds. Where once there were ash piles, now stood the clan members. Even the castle was restored.

"Everyone is back!" Luca exclaimed.

"Everyone?" Jasper looked down at Kato.

For a moment, there was nothing. Then Kato shifted his head in Jasper's arms. Jasper squeezed him.

"How is this possible?" Jasper looked up at Luca, who was now staring off behind Jasper. "Freya!" Jasper gasped, turning to look for her.

Freya's body lay sprawled on the ground. She had used all her energy to bring everyone back, but at what expense?

"Here, take him." Jasper carefully handed Kato to Luca. "I have to go check on her."

"Jasper?" Luca was shocked.

"It wasn't her that did this. It was Camille. She didn't deserve this." Jasper replied, looking deeply into Luca's eyes.

"Go." Luca nodded.

Jasper nodded back and took off to go check on Freya. Maybe there was a way to still save her.

"Freya?" Jasper knelt down, picking her up in his lap, "Freya, what have you done?"

"Hey," Freya smiled, looking up at Jasper, "I'll be fine."

"There has to be a way to help you." Jasper looked down at her, he could tell how drained she was.

"There is." She smiled, raising her closed hand to Japer's, "Let me go."

"What? Why?" Jasper gasped.

"I don't belong with you and your clan, especially after what I have done here tonight. Besides, maybe I will finally have a chance to meet my family." She continued to smile peacefully, "At least I was able to do one last good deed before I go." She nodded her head towards Jasper's hand.

"What do you mean?' Jasper asked, looking in his hand. He was holding the missing piece. "How?" he gasped, looking down to a lifeless Freya.

"Jasper, honey," Zara approached Jasper from behind, "she's gone."

"This isn't fair." Jasper wept as he held Freya in his arms.

"Life never is." Zara placed her hand on Jasper's shoulder, "She sacrificed herself for a miraculous cause." Zara looked at all the clan members that were once ash, but now full of life because of Freya, "Do not let her sacrifice be something that causes you not to continue to live. She wouldn't want that."

"People won't think of her as someone who sacrificed her life. They will all remember her as the one who attacked the village." Jasper shook his head.

"No, Jasper." Zara knelt down, "I, and the other Elders, will make sure she is remembered for this great gift she gave us. We will not let her be painted as the enemy. We are all aware of who that is."

"Camille." Jasper looked up at Zara, "I have to make her pay for this."

"We will help in any way we can." Zara grabbed Jasper and held him.

"What do we do with her now?" Jasper asked.

"Here," Zara waved at some clan's men to come over, "let them take her. We will have her cleaned up and give her a champion's burial. An honor bestowed on those who have made the greatest of sacrifices."

"Okay." Jasper nodded.

"Go to your dad." Zara wiped away the tears from Jasper's face. "You can help Luca and Axton get him somewhere for him to rest. He is going to need it."

"Thank you." Jasper smiled and gave Zara one last hug.

Jasper then walked over to his father, Luca, and Axton. They all worked together to pick Kato up and carried him into the castle. Kato would need to rest, but for how long was not known. Jasper looked back one last time as a group of men picked Freya up and carried her in the other direction.

CHAPTER NINETEEN

Kato remained unconscious for quite some time. He had been the only one who had not woken after Freya brought everyone back. The others were back up and doing their best to move past the events that had unfolded. Jasper had not left his father's side since the invasion. He even had Axton move an extra bed into Kato's room. Jasper assisted in taking care of him, patiently waiting for his dad to wake up. Jasper's patience was rewarded one morning while checking on Kato when his eyes began to open.

"Dad?" Jasper stood there, watching.

"Jasper?" Kato's eyes opened, "Is that you?"

"It's me, I'm right here." Jasper threw himself onto Kato hugging him tightly.

"How long have I been out?" He asked.

"You've been out for a couple of weeks now." Jasper said as he stood up and helped Kato sit up.

"What happened?" Kato rubbed his head, "I swear it felt like I died." He lightly laughed, but that laugh faded when Jasper replied.

"You did, dad." Jasper explained, "Freya was under Camille's influence and attacked our clan. When she broke free of her control, she used all of her energy to bring everyone she had killed back to life. It came at a steep price, though." Jasper looked down.

"Oh." Kato took Jasper's hand, "I'm sorry."

"It's okay, or at least it's getting there." Jasper looked up at Kato, "Life is full of bad things. That's what makes the good moments even better. She's with her family now. So, in a way, she got what she was searching for."

"Speaking of family," Kato looked at Jasper, "I think there's a lot we need to talk about."

"So, you still remember?" Jasper asked.

"I remember." Kato smiled.

"Good." Jasper was relieved, "I was worried, for a moment, that the memory block would return."

"I am sure you have many questions, and I will try to answer what I can. I can't, however, answer the one you want to know the most." Kato explained, "Jasper, the memory of your mom. Those memories are still blocked from me."

"I figured that already." Jasper chuckled, "I'm beginning to realize that mother of mine is a bit of a mystery." Jasper smiled at Kato, "She spoke to me, you know. Mom's voice came to me and told me I had the ability to make you remember."

"While I can't quite remember her, I can remember the love that radiated around her for you. She loved you so much. After all, someone wouldn't do what she did for you just because." Kato reached out for Jasper.

"I've come to realize the love that both of my parents have for me." Jasper leaned in and hugged Kato.

"Oh, he's awake." Zara's voice was full of excitement when she walked through the door. "I can come back in later." She said, noticing she interrupted them.

"No," Jasper laughed, letting go of Kato, "come on in."

"Zara?" Kato looked at her, "Zara, is it really you?"

"Oh, ha-ha." Zara laughed, "Did you guys practice this or something?"

"Zara. It's me, Kato." Kato said.

"I know who you are. You're Kato, the Chancellor." Zara walked closer to Kato and Jasper, stopping when Kato spoke.

"No." Kato became aggravated, "Why don't you re-member?" Then he looked at Jasper, "The memory block." He gasped, "You only removed it from me." Then he looked at Zara. "Jasper, do you think you can remove the block on Zara?"

"I mean, I can try. I've been working on my abilities while you've been resting." Jasper explained.

Jasper walked over to Zara and concentrated on removing the memory block put on her. Jasper channeled his energy and then touched his pointer finger against Zara's forehead, sending his energy rippling through her body. Zara backed away, batting her eyes and then stood still. She looked at Jasper and then Kato.

"Kato!" She exclaimed, rushing to his side.

"Zara." Kato smiled, embracing her.

"Wait?" Jasper stood there examining what was going down in front of him, "Is she…my–"

"No." Kato laughed, looking at Zara. Then his laugh faded as he looked at Jasper, "She's not your mother."

"Then who is she to you?" Jasper was confused.

"Like in the memories we had before the memory block was removed, she is a childhood friend of mine. She is also my most trusted ally from our home realm." Kato looked up at Zara.

"I stayed behind with him, when he chose to stay here. To help watch over you." Zara turned her gaze to Jasper. "I'm happy that you're safe," she looked back at Kato, "but, and I hate to down the mood, we have a lot to prepare for." she paused, "If Camille has already struck against us, then that means her memory is unlocking too. It's hard telling how much she remembers, possibly even more than us."

"Yes," Kato shook his head, "and we will discuss this. For now, though, let's enjoy this moment."

"Wait? So, what about Luca?" Jasper asked, "Is he like us? Or is he part of your cover here?"

"Yes," she laughed, "he's like us. Luca is really my son." Zara looked at Kato, "Both of our boys have grown into such strong men." Zara turned to Jasper, "Jasper, is there any way you can unblock his memories as well? He deserves to know about this all too." She asked, "I think he's with Axton right now."

Without hesitation, Jasper nodded, turned around, and ran out the door. Jasper ran to the main hall, looking for Axton and Luca. He found Axton but didn't see Luca with him.

"Axton," Jasper rushed to him, "where is Luca?"

"Oh, I left him in your room." Axton replied, "He said something about how it was only fair that he gets to go through your room after all the time you spent in his." Axton chuckled.

Jasper took off, running, heading straight for his room. He heard Axton yell behind him.

"Slow down! Stop running. You're going to hurt yourself."

Jasper disregarded Axton's commands and continued on to his room. He was on a mission. Jasper rounded his doorway, coming to a standstill. He saw Luca standing in front of his bed. He seemed to be reading one of the books that Jasper had set on his bedside table. Luca turned around, jumping when he saw Jasper.

"Huh." Luca sighed, "Ratted out by the castle. Well, that's a first." He smirked, "At least I got a few moments to snoop through your stuff."

Jasper didn't speak, he just stared directly at Luca. They hadn't seen each other much since their shared kiss. Jasper had been too preoccupied with Kato. Now that Kato was settled, though, Jasper could bring his focus to setting things straight.

Luca wore a plain white shirt and ripped jeans. Jasper took in the other details of Luca. His hair waved messily down his head. His amber eyes staring back at Jasper. The way his smiling lips perfectly curved, showing just a hint of his teeth. Jasper walked closer to him.

"What?" Luca gave a nervous laugh.

Jasper reached out and grabbed Luca, bringing Luca's body against his. Jasper looked deeply into Luca's eyes, noticing the way Luca was staring at him. Jasper had caught Luca off guard, and he enjoyed that. Jasper's heart began to beat faster as he reached out and moved Luca's hair out his face.

Jasper pulled Luca even closer, feeling Luca's body quiver to his touch. Then with a smile, Jasper went in for the kiss. Jasper noticed Luca's body jolted, the way his did when Luca had kissed him. Jasper felt Luca's hands on his sides. He shivered, as Luca slowly slid them up his back to hold him. Luca pulled his head away and looked back into Jasper's eyes.

"Took you long enough" Luca smiled.

"Oh," Jasper smirked, "I'm just starting. You haven't seen anything yet."

Jasper pulled Luca back in. This time as he kissed him, Jasper allowed some of his energy to flow through his lips and into Luca. This caused Luca to jump back.

"What, what was that?" Luca asked, lightly brushing his fingers against his lips.

Jasper watched as his energy took effect and unlocked

the memory block put upon Luca. He stood still as Luca registered what this all meant.

"Wait." Luca paused, "Am I like you?"

"I guess we have more in common than we thought." Jasper walked towards Luca, "We have a lot to talk about."

"We do," Luca pulled Jasper close, pressing his body against Jasper's, "but that can wait. I believe we were in the middle of something."

"Oh?" Jasper asked with a smirk, "Maybe you could remind me?"

"My pleasure." Luca grinned as he tightly wrapped his arms around Jasper and began kissing him.

They stood there for what felt like an eternity. Just holding one another and giving in to long-denied emotions. Jasper didn't want it to stop. Jasper nudged his body closer to Luca's, wanting there to be no space between them. This caused Luca to lose his balance and for them both to fall onto Jasper's bed. They both laughed but didn't let that stop them. They continued grabbing each other, rolling all over the bed.

"Well," Axton stood in the doorway, "I guess you found him."

"Oh, Axton." Jasper said as he and Luca sat up.

"Oh, don't let me interrupt." Axton smirked, "After all, I was always team Luca." He winked, then turned and left the room.

Jasper and Luca turned and looked at each other. They broke out in laughter while falling back on the bed.

"What now?" Luca asked.

"I have a few ideas," Jasper smiled, fixing his hair out of his face. Then slid his hand through Luca's hair, moving it out of his face too, "but we should probably take you to your mom. Something tells me she wants to see you."

Luca sighed, but he nodded in agreement. The boys got up and headed to Kato's room. While they were at it, the boys filled their parents in about their newfound relationship.

"Well," Kato looked at Zara, "it sure took them long enough."

"You're telling me." Zara laughed.

"Sounds like everyone was team Luca." Jasper chuckled, nudging Luca.

They all laughed and spent the evening just enjoying each other's company. It was a much needed evening. When it was time for Zara to leave, Luca stopped her and asked permission to stay behind with Jasper. Kato and Zara approved, and let him stay. Luca gave his mom a hug and told her bye while Jasper gave his dad a hug too. Then both boys headed off to Jasper's room to get ready for bed.

Luca took a shower and got changed for the night. Once he was finished, Jasper got ready for a shower of his own. It was relaxing, in a way, to take a shower in his own bathroom. Though he had been in the castle for weeks now, he had been using Kato's shower so he could stay within range of his father. Using his own bathroom carried its own serenity to it. Jasper walked out of the bathroom, wrapped in a towel.

"I want so bad to make a joke about grabbing an extra cover." Jasper grinned, grabbing his towel, "But I don't want to come off too easy." He let the towel fall to the floor, revealing he was wearing boxers.

"You're silly." Luca chuckled, "Climb on in." Luca raised the cover for Jasper, showing he was in the same.

"Okay," Jasper laughed, "but I wasn't kidding. Don't go getting any ideas, I'm a real gentleman." He teased as he climbed under the covers nuzzling up to Luca.

"That works for me." Luca smiled, grabbing Jasper and pulling him in.

They cuddled up against one another. While there was more that they needed to figure out and prepare for, Jasper, for the first time in a long time, wasn't going to worry about that right now. For now, he was going to block all of that out of his mind and enjoy the piece of bliss he had in this moment. Luca and Jasper held each other close until they both drifted off to sleep. For Jasper, life was good.

The boys had been asleep for a couple hours when Jasper began tossing and turning in his sleep. Luca woke and tried calming him down, but to no avail. Jasper's body jolted, causing him to sit straight up. He was covered in sweat. Luca sat up next to him, trying to get him to speak.

"Jasper?" Luca tried getting his attention, "What's wrong?"

"It's Freya." Jasper turned his head and looked at Luca, "We have to save her."

Acknowledgements

To those who supported and cheered me on, I thank you. I could not have gotten this far without the help you gave. I am more grateful than you may ever know.

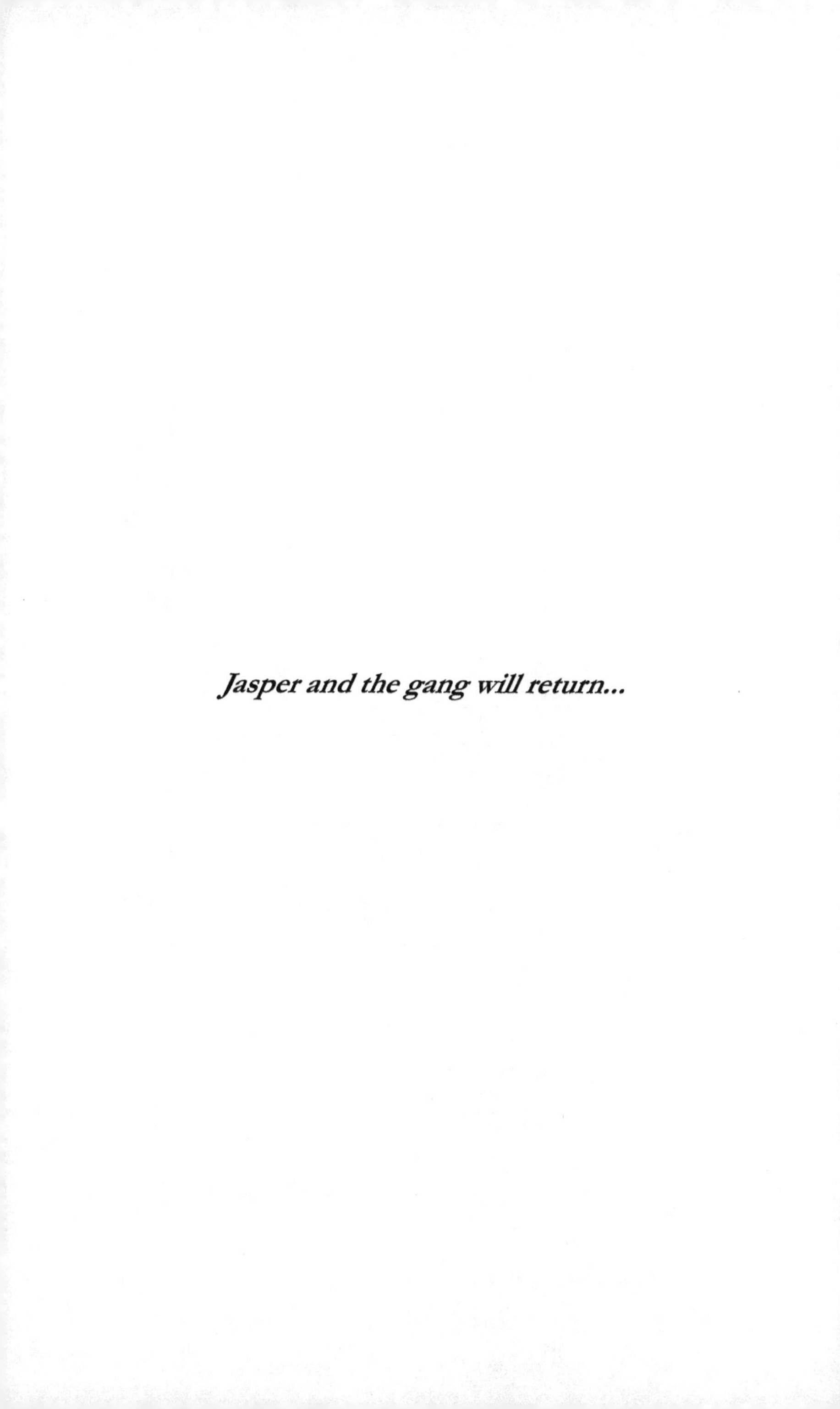

Jasper and the gang will return...